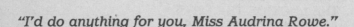

"I'd do anything for you, Miss Audrina Rowe."

Then she was in his arms. No, Max told himself, it was only gratitude. Besides, she was too small. He'd get a crick in his neck. But Miss Rowe must have stood on tiptoe and raised her face along with her arms, pulling his mouth down to hers, for now she felt just right. He was tasting the champagne on her soft, willing lips, and feeling her sweet body pressed against his. And that felt just right, too. . . .

VALENTINES

A Trio of Regency Love Stories
for Sweethearts' Day

Barbara Metzger

FAWCETT CREST • NEW YORK

A Fawcett Crest Book
Published by Ballantine Books
Copyright © 1996 by Barbara Metzger

All rights reserved under International and Pan-American Copyright Conventions. Published in the United States by Ballantine Books, a division of Random House, Inc., New York, and simultaneously in Canada by Random House of Canada Limited, Toronto.

Library of Congress Catalog Card Number: 95-90701

ISBN 0-449-22352-3

Manufactured in the United States of America

First Edition: February 1996

10 9 8 7 6 5 4 3 2 1

To Mr. and Mrs. Neal Pruzan in honor of their wedding.
I should have been there.
Congratulations and Happy Anniversary

Contents

Bald Lies

Chapter One

There was fog. There was the dark of night. There was smoke from candles and smudge from cigars. Mostly, however, there was a cloud of gloom hanging over the corner table at White's Club that cold January evening.

Three friends sat slumped around the table, each too deep in despair to notice the card games going on around them, the wagering or the tongue-wagging. No acquaintances stopped by with offers of a hand of whist, or for opinions on a fine piece of horseflesh, or comments on the finer flesh of the new horseback rider at Astley's. Only the silent waiters dared approach, with bottle after bottle of liquor. There was enough brandy splashed that night to flambé an entire cherry orchard. There was enough melancholy to produce *Hamlet* thrice over.

Other than the maudlin pall, the three gentlemen shared little in common at first glance. One was a veteran of the Peninsula campaign, a tanned and hardened Corinthian. One was a leading light in his party's political future, solid and comfortable. One was a Tulip, with pomaded locks and yellow cossack trousers. His shirt points were so high, he would have been blinded had he chosen to examine anything but the wet ring his glass was leaving on the table.

The gentlemen did share a dawning familiarity with three decades of life, and all were peers of the realm: an earl, a viscount, and a baron. And they were best of friends since schoolboy days, pulling each other through scrapes and Suetonius, sharing vacations, allowances, and confidences. Now they were well past adolescent pranks, but they still shared each other's woes.

Gordon, Viscount Halbersham, was the first to speak. The young Whig reformer cleared his throat, almost as if he were about to address the House of Lords. Instead of his usual ringing Parliamentary tones, though, he uttered a pitiful whine: "I think Vi is having an affair."

Neither of his friends disputed him. Neither pair of eyes could meet his. How could they deny his wife was cuckolding him, when it was the talk of London? There were wagers entered in White's own betting book to that effect.

"And with Fitzroy-Hughes, of all men!" the viscount went on, more to himself than to his unresponsive tablemates. "A blasted Tory."

"He dresses well," put in Lord Frances Podell, the fashionable but drooping baron.

"Now, that's a fine lot of sympathy, Franny." Viscount Halbersham rounded on his foppish friend. "Very helpful." He swallowed another glass of brandy. "Damn, what's a man to expect from such a fribble? Orange and purple butterflies on your waistcoat, by George. It's a miracle you weren't set upon by some wild-eyed lepidopterist."

Franny ignored the slur, knowing Gordon only spoke from his own despondency—and poor taste. "Then run the dastard through and be done with it."

"What, and have to flee the country? We're at war with every place worth visiting. Of course, there are the

4

Antipodes. A duel would put paid to my career anyway."

Another silence ensued until Maxim, the Earl of Blanford, lifted his dark eyes from the contemplation of his own personal hell in the bottom of his brandy glass. "Come now, Gordie, things can't be as bad as all that. You don't know for sure Lady Viola is playing you false. Just because she made sure Fitzroy-Hughes was invited to that New Year's house party is no reason to suspect the worst."

"She did dance with him a lot," Franny put in, earning glares from both men.

"But you don't like to dance, Gordie," Lord Blanford offered. "And Lady Vi does."

"They both disappeared for an hour during the ball."

The earl brushed that aside. "Coincidence only."

"She kissed him at twelve o'clock."

"You were across the room."

"I caught him wandering down the wrong hall that night."

"Have you considered Jamaica? I hear the scenery is nice, but the climate . . ."

They all had another drink.

"Deuce take it," Blanford eventually said. "There has to be another way. Why the devil don't you get the chit pregnant already? Motherhood will settle her down well enough. It works for broody mares. Get her mind off anything but filling her nursery. You've been married, what? Two years now since we stood up with you. What in blazes have you been doing?"

"I guess we all know what he hasn't been doing," Franny put in, "if Lady Vi's making sheep's eyes at Fitzroy-Hughes."

"Confound it, it ain't my fault!" Lord Halbersham exploded. "She's off at some ball or rout or theater party till dawn, then she's asleep till midday, when I've got to be at the House. By the time I get home, she's dressing for another blasted outing, and it's 'Oh no,

Gordie, you'll muss my gown,' or 'Sorry, Gordie, my maid has already done my hair.' Women, bah!"

Max was studying his fingertips. "I don't think it's women as much as London. It sounds like the social rounds are your real competition. Lady Vi is a beautiful little baggage; that's why you married her in the first place. But if not Fitzroy-Hughes—and I'm not saying he is poaching on your preserves—then you'll be worrying over someone else soon enough. Best to get the minx out of Town altogether. Spend some time together at your country place, work on propagating the species and extending the line, all that rot. You've been talking about setting up a stud farm for years. Tell Viola you're going to do it now, as an excuse for ruralizing."

"Things are slow in Town now anyway. The real parties won't start up again until the spring," Franny added.

"And you said yourself things are quiet at Whitehall with so many members in the shires over the winter."

The viscount's brow cleared for a minute, then the frown lines returned. "Vi hates the country. She won't go."

"Confound it, man, she's your wife. She doesn't have a choice."

"Spoken like a real bachelor," Halbersham replied. "You believe all that legal argle-bargle of a wife being man's chattel, and that oath stuff about her swearing to honor and obey. It's a hum, all of it. Wives have ways of getting what they want, let me tell you. Cold meals, overstarched linen, exorbitant dressmakers' bills. That's just the start! Then there are the tears. No, Max, a wise man doesn't start ordering his wife around like some kind of servant, making her do what she doesn't want. Viola would make my life hell."

"Seems to me," pronounced Lord Blanford, watching his friend sink back into his dolorous stupor, "that she's already got you halfway there."

6

Viscount Halbersham took a deep swallow of oblivion, and another when the first wasn't working.

It was Lord Podell who spoke next, after a few moments of reflection on his companion's sorry state, and his own. "Seems to me it would be cheaper, too," he said.

"What, a duel? Are you still of a mind to second me at dawn then? Deuce take a fellow if his own friends are so anxious for his blood."

"No, I meant the country. Got to be a sight less costly than Town. Why, no one would care if a chap wore the same waistcoat to dinner twice in a week."

"They would if it was one like yours," Gordie muttered, but Max shook himself out of his own doldrums to take a careful look at his dandified friend. Between Podell's intricate neckcloth and curling-tonged tresses were worry lines, sleepless shadows. "What, dipped again, Franny?" He started to reach for his purse. It was no secret the baron was punting on River Tick.

Franny held up a manicured hand. "Thanks, but it's bellows to mend with me. A loan won't cover it this time, and a fellow can't keep borrowing from his friends, especially when he knows he's got no way to pay them back. Mightn't have a brass farthing, but I've got m'honor."

"Don't be a gudgeon, Fran. Surely a monkey will see you through. You'll come about, old son, and Max will never notice the loss," Gordie volunteered. "Rich as Golden Ball, our boy Blanford." The viscount peered through a drunken haze at his somber friend. "I say, Max, you ain't lost your fortune, too, have you? Mean to say, here you are, blue-deviled as the two of us, and you ain't even got a wife."

Max just shook his head, his hand still poised at his waistcoat pocket and one eyebrow raised in inquiry toward Podell.

Franny had to repeat, "It won't fadge, Max. You might buy the duns away from my door today, but what

7

about tomorrow? We all know the dibs are never going to be in tune."

Gordon lifted his quizzing glass in an unsteady grip, but still managed to get a better look at Lord Podell's ensemble. "Dash it, Franny, if you didn't spend all your blunt on some Bedlamite tailor, you might have enough put by for the rent."

Franny sniffed. "A fellow has to keep up appearances, don't you know."

"Maybe you should consider going to the country for a while after all," Max suggested. "As you said, the pigs and sheep won't care if your outfit is bang up to the mark."

"Outrun the bailiffs, you mean." Franny gave a dry laugh. "I would if I could. But the Hall is leased out, don't you know. The rent money is the only thing paying the mortgage, else the cents-per-centers would have the ancestral heap, too. The rent's not enough to cover improvements to the land, though, and without some major investment, new equipment, better conditions for the tenants, I can't turn a profit."

Gordon nodded. His wealth came from the land, too. "Surprised you managed to hold on to the place this long, in the condition you inherited it."

Franny sat up a little straighter. "It's been in the family for centuries."

"It was your father's family home, too. Forgive me for speaking ill of the dead, but he didn't seem to give a groat about the place."

Franny sank back into his chair, and into his misery. "Gambling fever. Fatal flaw, don't you know."

Gordon snorted. "Fatal is one thing, foolish is another. Spending your last shillings on silver buttons."

Franny started to say that the buttons weren't paid for when Max spoke up: "What you need, Franny, is a wife."

"What, after Gordie's tale of woe as recommendation? No, thank you. I'd rather go to debtors' prison."

"Stubble it, I don't mean a wife like Gordie's."

Gordie was on his feet. "Now, wait a minute—"

Max waved him down. "No insult intended. Lady Halbersham is a diamond of the first water, a Toast since her come-out. But there's no getting around that she's an expensive piece of goods. That's not what Franny needs. He needs an heiress."

Franny managed a shaky laugh. "Then I'm safe. Heiresses are watched as carefully as eggs on a griddle. No rich papa's going to let any down-at-heels baron within a mile of his precious daughter. 'Sides, I ain't in the petticoat line."

Max ignored the last, and continued his deliberations out loud while Gordon nodded sagely. "Not an heiress of the *beau monde* then—"

"Hold on, I ain't about to buckle myself to some Cit's platter-faced gal just so she can call herself baroness and try to drag her family into the ton on my coattails."

"No, that's not what you need. Gordie had to have a wife with elegance, social standing, a regular darling of the nobility to be his perfect political hostess." He raised his glass in a toast to Halbersham's absent, if erring, wife. "You need a wealthy chit from the gentry who's used to the country and won't mind staying there. You install her and her papa's money at the Hall, give the old man a grandson to call heir to a barony, and you are free to take up your London life right where you left off."

"Here, here," Gordie seconded.

"But I ain't in the petticoat line, I tell you," Franny said in a near whimper.

Once again he was ignored. Max was staring at the ceiling through a smoke ring he'd blown. "In fact, you ought to go on home to Bedford with Gordie and Lady Vi. Get you away from your creditors for a time, and a chance to look at the crop of local beauties before they

9

make their bows in Town and get spoiled by city ways."

Gordie wasn't sure if his wife had been insulted again. He was so far in his cups, he wasn't sure of anything except that he might have a chance of convincing Viola to accompany him to the country if they made a house party out of it. "There's nothing Vi likes better than matchmaking," he said, toasting the earl's brilliance with another glass. "We'll do it!"

After a few more glasses, even Franny began to see the merits of the plan. What other choice did he have? He swallowed, and nodded.

Gordie slapped him on the back. "That's the ticket. You'll see, we'll all come about." He stood to leave, anxious to confront his wife while his enthusiasm—and courage—were high. Before he left, offering Franny a ride in his coach, he turned to the earl. "I say, Max, why don't you come along? We can get in some shooting and you can help keep Vi from missing the pleasures of Town. Besides, I really do mean to set up the stud, and there's no better judge of horseflesh than you."

"And you know I'll be bound to make mice feet of any courtship. Need your advice," Franny declared firmly, more firm than his wavering stance, held up by his sturdier friend. "Not in the petticoat line."

Max waved them on. "I'll think about it."

"You do that." Gordon turned to go again, half dragging Franny. He stopped at the edge of the table, temporarily propping his lordship against a passing footman, to whom Franny was confiding his anxieties about the female species, to the fellow's disgust and horror. "Oh, by the by," Gordon said, "never did get to ask what had you so moped. I mean, what are friends for, if not to listen to a chap's troubles?"

Lord Blanford merely raised his glass again in acknowledgment. "Go on, get Franny home before he is arrested. It's nothing worth mentioning anyway."

Max poured himself another glassful, alone there in the corner. Nothing worth mentioning, right? His life was over, that was all, but no, it wasn't worth mentioning.

Chapter Two

Max could not have opened his budget to Gordon or Franny anyway. His problem was not something to discuss even with one's best friends; they couldn't understand, not having the same experience. Besides, it was so terrible, so personal, so blasted depressing, Max didn't want to talk about it. Gordie's marriage was in peril and poor Franny's finances were at *point non plus*, earning them both his sympathy and compassion . . . but he, Maxim Blanding, Earl of Blanford, late of His Majesty's Cavalry, was going bald.

Oh Lord, bald! His hair wasn't just receding, it was retreating with the lightning speed of one of Wellesley's tactical withdrawals. At this rate, he'd be— No, it didn't bear contemplating.

Max told himself, not for the first time, that it wasn't just vanity that made him wince with every hair left in the teeth of his comb. He never thought his looks were much of an asset in the first place, with a crooked nose from a long-forgotten cricket match and new scars from the more recent army days. Always dark-complexioned, he now had a weathered appearance, like an unpainted shutter.

The incipient resemblance to a hen's offering didn't

even bother Max as a *memento mori*. He'd faced death on the battlefield often enough to accept his own mortality. No, he saw each fall of dark thread, each ebony remnant on his pillow slip, as a sign of betrayal. His body was playing him false by growing old. Old. Max Blanding, first cricketer, Lieutenant Lord Blanford—growing old? How had that happened? He was only two and thirty. He couldn't be old yet.

Max had studied his friends this evening, searching for signs of decay. Gordie was gaining some girth, but he was still the rosy-cheeked lad from school days. And Franny, despite his affectations in dress, was still a blond, blue-eyed cherub. They were all of an age, so how was Max the only one getting old?

He pondered the question while he waited for the footman to bring another bottle to the table. At this rate, he estimated, in less than a decade his teeth would be coming loose and his stomach would be straining toward his knees, no matter how hard he worked at Gentleman Jackson's. He sucked in those muscles with a gasp.

"Are you all right, my lord?" the worried servant asked.

Max scowled the waiter away. He didn't feel old, that was the rub. Gordie could settle into middle age with his career and his flighty wife; Max wasn't ready. Perhaps because he'd given three years to Wellesley's campaign, he felt cheated. There was too much he hadn't done, like secure his own succession, for one. Here he was chiding Gordie, and he had naught but a chinless cousin to inherit. He'd thought to have plenty of time, at least until he was forty, before starting his nursery. Now who knew how soon before he lost that, too? Zeus, by the time he found a suitable bride, he'd likely be wearing whalebone corsets and ivory teeth. Held together by dead creatures, by George, he'd creak when he stooped to one knee to make his offer, and have to be helped up by some smirking chit who'd have to shout her acceptance into his ear trumpet.

Not that Max doubted she'd accept, whichever woman he chose to bear his sons. He was still an earl with deep pockets, no matter that he was nearing his dotage. Unfortunately, he was enough of the dreamer to regret being accepted for his title and wealth alone. Name, fortune, and an acceptable appearance made a much better bargain. A shiny pate was no more acceptable to Maxim than stains on his linen.

He sighed. Perhaps he should take the advice he'd so blithely offered to Franny and find himself a comfortable wife now, while there were still strands long enough to pull across his forehead. Hair today, groom tomorrow.

The glittering London belles held no appeal for him. He'd dread seeing his scalp reflected back in his fashionable wife's cold, disapproving eyes. No, he'd think about going into the country with his friends to look over the provincial possibilities—tomorrow. For tonight he had to concentrate on getting home without looking like he couldn't hold his liquor anymore, either.

He made it across the floor without mishap, and waited with studied nonchalance for the doorman to hand over his hat and gloves.

"Best to bundle up, my lord," the man offered with a smile. "It's cold enough out there to freeze the whiskers off a rat."

Hair jokes? Was he now to be the butt of hair jokes? Lord Blanford changed the doorman's tip to a smaller coin, crammed his curly-brimmed beaver down over his ears, and stalked off into the night.

Gordon, Lord Halbersham, managed to convince his pretty young wife to leave the gaiety of the capital without too much effort. Viola was already contemplating a visit to Bedfordshire anyway, with London so thin of company. With all those starchy dowagers giving

14

her gimlet looks, Viola thought she'd do well to let memories of that New Year's party fade a bit lest she find certain doors closed to her at the start of the real Season.

So Gordie merely had to promise her a new set of diamonds, the refurbishment of Briarwoods, his country seat, in time for a lavish Valentine's Day ball, and the management of Lord Frances Podell's love life.

"Let me see. There's Lord Craymore's daughter. Ten thousand a year. She's been on the shelf so long, even Franny's empty pockets should look good." She chewed on the stub of her pencil, adding names to the list. "That awful Mr. Martin's girl should be out by now. He's in trade, rich as Croesus, but the mother was acceptable. And Pamela Feswick is always on the lookout for a husband."

"Dash it, Vi, the Feswick woman is thirty if she's a day, and a shrew. Think of poor Franny."

"Exactly. Poor. And awkward around strange women."

"That Feswick woman is as strange as they come. Remember we'll have to entertain them now and again. Don't mean to give up Franny's friendship."

Pamela Feswick was crossed off the list. "Too bad it's not Blanford looking for a wife. There'd be no trouble there finding any number of acceptable girls." And her house party would be the most notable success of the year, instead of being a humiliating repairing lease.

Gordie laughed. "There have been acceptable and not-so-acceptable females throwing themselves at Max's head since he was out of short pants. He wouldn't need us to find him a bride, were he looking to get legshackled. Which he ain't, so don't get that look in your eye. Max ain't one to put up with anyone meddling in his personal life."

"Still, if he came, we could attract more women for Franny to look over. Max is definitely a prize worth pursuing, even if he doesn't permit himself to be caught."

"Dash it, I hate having my friends put up as bait."

"And I hate your making marriage out to be a fate worse than death," she replied with a scowl.

Gordie cleared his throat and made a strategic retreat. "Not at all, my dear. Not at all. It's just that Max will do what he wants to do. Always has. Went and joined the army, didn't he, even though he was the old earl's heir? No, you worry about Franny." His lordship meandered about the sitting room between their bedchambers. "Ah, Vi, it's late. You can fret about the party tomorrow. Why don't you, ah, come along to bed now?"

Viola shooed him off with an absentminded wave of her beringed fingers. "You go on, Gordie. I'm going to write an invitation to Max begging him to come. For Franny's sake."

Viola's note reached Max about noontime the next day, along with his morning coffee.

"Are we ready to arise, my lord?" his valet inquired.

"We are ready for the last rites, Thistlewaite," Max groaned from the depths of a pounding headache. He was definitely too old for this.

Thistlewaite left to return with a potent, noxious-smelling brew calculated to cure hangovers, or kill the sufferer. "Drink up, my lord. We'll feel more the thing after a shave."

Only if he could hold the razor to Thistlewaite's throat, Max thought, but he drank while the valet bustled about with hot water and lather. Thistlewaite had been in the family forever, like the suits of armor in the hall. The man was about as companionable as those clanking hulks, but Max could no more get rid of the servant than he could sell off the family plate. He'd tried. Thistlewaite wouldn't go, looking after the Earls of Blanford being his God-given mission in life, according to Thistlewaite. At least he gave a good shave.

While dabbing warm lather on the earl's face,

16

Thistlewaite asked, "Shall we be exercising at Gentleman Jackson's Boxing Saloon this afternoon, my lord?"

"*I* shall be going a few rounds with the Gentleman himself. *You* shall start packing." He indicated the invitation he'd set aside as the valet approached with the razor. "I am thinking of joining Lord and Lady Halbersham at their Bedfordshire property."

Making firm, even strokes, Thistlewaite commented, "Very good, my lord. Lord Podell will be relieved. He called earlier this morning to discuss the invitation."

"And what did you tell him?"

"That we hadn't decided yet, but it was an excellent idea."

"What, getting him out of Town?"

Thistlewaite was applying the damp towel now. "No, finding him a wealthy bride. When a gentleman reaches a certain age, he owes it to his lineage to—"

"Please, Thistlewaite, no lectures this morning."

"Very good, my lord." The valet replaced the towel and other equipment on the shaving stand. "Perhaps a bit of boot polish would do."

Max sat up, too suddenly for his aching head. "What the devil . . . ?"

"Here, this bare spot in the back. If we cover it with blacking, perhaps no one will notice."

Max jumped up and craned his neck around toward the mirror. "The back? You mean there's a bare spot on the back, too, not just the receding hairline?"

Thistlewaite silently held up a hand mirror so the earl could see his back's reflection. "Oh Lud." He sank back into his chair.

"The boot polish, my lord?"

"What, and have it drip down my back as soon as I break a sweat at Jackson's? No, just comb it across as best you can," Max said with resignation.

"Very good, my lord. I suppose we cannot consider some rice powder for the, ah, forehead then, to take away the shine?"

Max grabbed for the mirror again. "Shine? There's no blasted shine. It's the light, that's all."

Thistlewaite stared at the wall behind his employer. "When a gentleman reaches a certain age . . ."

"I know, I know! Dash it, I've already decided to look around at the available chits Lady Halbersham trots out for Franny. Better get the job done while I still have some grass in the meadow."

"Excellent plan, my lord. There are some fine country families in Bedford."

Max stood up to have his coat fitted across his broad shoulders. "I'm glad you approve. For a moment I was worried you'd hold out for a bride from the social columns, some starched-up aristocrat."

Thistlewaite brushed at the sleeves. "Since a dowry is not the first consideration, although not to be disdained if one is available, character is more important in our countess. A kind heart, a loving nature."

Those were more or less the requirements Max had arrived at, since he'd not yet stumbled across a woman who inspired eternal devotion. Of course, he couldn't admit to his valet that he was willing to settle for comfort instead of passion. "Why, Thistlewaite, you old dog you, I didn't know you had such a soft streak. I thought you'd have me make one of those dynastic arranged marriages of titles, lands, and money. Lud knows you've been nattering on about this debutante ball or that duke's daughter for ages."

"Exactly, my lord. And nothing came of it."

"Oh, so now you are willing to accept a lesser mortal, to see me in parson's mousetrap. Female, fertile and friendly, that's all, eh? Well, I suppose a fellow could do worse." Max gave one last swipe of the comb across his head, then looked longingly at the hairs left in the comb's teeth. "A lot worse."

Thistlewaite followed his eyes. "Perhaps it is time to consider a hairpiece, my lord."

"What, a wig?" Max practically shouted. "Never!"

"Not an old-fashioned full wig, just a subtle addition to your own hair. The ladies do it all the time, with false curls or added braids for height."

"Good grief, I'm not that vain, man."

"But we do have an appearance to maintain. It's not like buckram wadding to broaden our shoulders, or, heaven forfend, sawdust to pad our calves. We have no need to resort to such subterfuges. But a discreet bit of hair . . ."

"Dash it, I'm not going to wear a dead rat on my head! I'd be the laughingstock of London."

"In London, perhaps, but in Bedfordshire, where no one knows us? 'Twould make a better impression on the young ladies."

Max thought of some sweet young female cringing at his looks, forced by her family to accept his suit. "So I make a better impression. What happens after the wedding night when my new little wife goes to run her fingers through my hair? Surprise, sweetheart, your husband is as bald as a baby's behind?"

Thistlewaite clucked his tongue. "We wear a nightcap for a month or two until she grows used to it."

"Blast it, *we*'re not getting into bed with some silly chit who's going to set up a screech when she finds she's married a plucked goose. I am!" Max snatched up his gloves and headed toward the door. His last glimpse was of Thistlewaite pulling hairs out of his brush, shaking his head. "Deuce take it, I'll think about it. But don't go cutting off the tails of my horses."

Chapter Three

*B*achelors in the neighborhood! Bachelors in the neighborhood! It didn't have quite the ring of "For God, King, and Country," but as far as battle calls, it was an effective rally cry. Every proud mama in Bedford, every despairing papa, took note as soon as Lady Halbersham's instructions were delivered to her housekeeper at Briarwoods, the Halbersham estate.

The housekeeper had a cousin, the butler had a crony at the Spotted Dog. A footman was walking out with a maid at Squire's place, and the potboy went home to his mum in the village at night. Every servant in the county soon knew Lady Viola's plans, and every cottager, local merchant, and so on, until word reached those most interested, the wellborn or well-to-do—and their daughters. In the country where every eligible *parti* was known since leading strings, strange gentlemen were noteworthy indeed, especially if they happened to be London swells.

From Lady Halbersham's designations of the rooms to be aired, it was understood that Lord Halbersham's boon companions were to attend. The usual sources—afternoon teas, whispered conferences at the lending library, hasty searches through the back issues of social columns—immediately ascertained that the higher-ranking Lord Blanford was a top-of-the-trees Corinthian, and a confirmed bachelor. No matter. No one is more hopeful than the mother of a pretty girl. That he was reputed to be something of a rake merely added spice. Lord Podell was said to be most unfortunately pockets-to-let, likely on the lookout for an heiress. The poorer girls sighed, for the baron was reportedly as handsome as he could stare. Still, there were bound to be parties and dinners, and even a ball to look forward to in the middle of winter.

Parents started praying, dressmakers started stitching. The local merchants and draymen all found cause to toast Lord Halbersham and his friends. The house party was a success before anyone arrived.

And to Miss Audrina Rowe, it was a godsend. She'd heard at the little vicarage where she called every day to wish her father good morning and make sure Mrs. Dodd had his breakfast eggs cooked just the way he wished. Mrs. Dodd knew all about the house party, from her nevvy who was groom at Briarwoods Manor. Jem Cochlin, delivering the bread, added his bits of information, and even young Master Timothy from Squire's come for his Latin lesson was bursting with the news.

While Audrina was helping Vicar Rowe with his sermon, they even discussed if he should write in a welcome to the strangers to the congregation, for he was liable to forget without his notes.

"I'm not sure such fine London gentlemen will attend our tiny village chapel, Papa. From what I hear, they are not precisely the devout types." Her mind was already full of scraps about gambling, drinking, womanizing, horse-racing. "No, I do not expect to see them in St. Margaret's."

The vicar patted his beloved daughter on the hand. "Now, Audrina, we mustn't listen to gossip, you know, or prejudge guests to our community. I'm sure our Lord Halbersham only knows fine, upstanding gentlemen."

Since anyone, even his eighteen-year-old daughter who'd never been farther afield than an assembly in Upper Throckton, was more worldly than Vicar Rowe, his opinion was suspect. Dree wanted to disagree, but she knew better than to argue with her father, who'd find some good in Lucifer himself. She merely kissed the vicar good-bye.

"Yes, hurry along, Audrina. I'm sure your cousin Carinne will be needing you."

No, Carinne didn't need Dree, except to hand over fresh handkerchiefs to mop up her tears. What Carrie needed was a miracle, and Dree might just have found it—or him. Audrina didn't care if those London toffs were pagan fire-worshipers or peep-o'-day boys. They were young and titled. Either one had to make Carinne a better husband than Lord Prendergast. Now all she had to do was convince Carinne's father, Uncle Augustus Martin, of the fact.

On her way back to White Oaks, her uncle's estate, Dree pondered ways to convince him, since Uncle Augustus was even more set in his opinions than dear Papa. Papa could never hold with thinking ill of anyone; Mr. Martin could never hold with anyone else's thinking, particularly not a female, and a harum-scarum young female to boot. Audrina reminded herself to try to put her flyaway hair in some kind of order before scratching on the door of his library. She shuddered, and not from the cold winter wind.

That library was where Uncle Augustus was wont to shout at servants, scold his daughter, and upbraid his niece for Carinne's shortcomings, as if Dree could make her dear cousin into anything but the loveliest, sweetest girl in all of Bedfordshire. No, Audrina Rowe did not want to face her foul-tempered uncle, but she would, for Carrie's sake.

How could she not, when she owed her cousin so much? Why, the warm cloak she wore right now was a gift, as was the made-over dress she had under it. Dree could never forget the broths and healthful foods Carrie sent down to the vicarage when Papa was so sick last year, and how sometimes she'd sent Dree a coin or two, from her pin money, she said, because the vicar would give his income away in charity. And she did it all despite the wishes of a father she was petrified of, a man who didn't have an ounce of charity in him.

Uncle Augustus gave Audrina room and board now, not out of the goodness of his heart, but so he wouldn't have to hire a companion for his daughter. Not that Dree could show her older cousin how to go on; the fancy boarding school Carrie had attended was supposed to have accomplished that. Dree's purpose was to satisfy conventions, that Mr. Martin's daughter was not traipsing unchaperoned about the countryside like a hoyden. The fact that his niece had to complete the two-mile walk any time she wished to check on Papa mattered naught to Mr. Martin, certainly not enough to permit one of his footmen to accompany her, or a groom to hitch up a pony cart for her. Dree kicked a rock out of her way. She supposed she should be grateful he didn't put her to work mucking out the stalls on the stableboys' half days off. As it was, she already helped the housekeeper with the mending and the butler with the polishing, menial jobs Carrie was never permitted to do as they were considered less than ladylike.

Audrina didn't mind, really, since this was the least hard she'd ever worked in her life. And she did feel lucky to be close to her cousin while helping Papa with the pittance Uncle Augustus gave her, instead of tending someone's spoiled children or testy grandmother. Besides, she'd promised her aunt when that lady passed on that she'd stand Carinne's friend, for Aunt Estelle knew that her sweet-natured daughter would never be able to stand up to Augustus Martin. No one did.

Aunt Estelle and Audrina's own mama were sisters, but what different paths their lives had taken. They were pampered daughters of a marquis, but one with six

23

girls to marry off, and precious little interest in providing them dowries. Aunt Estelle was bartered into an arranged marriage to the head of the Martin Shipbuilding firm in Portsmouth, who wanted the noble connection enough to come down handsomely for his bride. He grew bitter when he realized his wellborn bride brought him nothing but cuts, even from her own family. Dree believed he shouted Aunt Estelle into an early grave.

Audrina's own mother refused to wed the man her father chose, instead running off with the young vicar. She was happy, except for never seeing any of her family again. They disowned her as quickly as they repudiated the daughter with a husband in trade. Mama had died from exhaustion and lack of medical care, despite unanswered pleas to the current marquis, her own brother. Dree did not have much esteem for the nobility.

Not so Uncle Augustus, who was determined to have his daughter rise where he could not, to show those blasted in-laws of his. His birth couldn't open aristocracy's door a crack; his fortune could. Dree didn't think much of wealth either, if it could only buy the likes of Lord Prendergast.

Prendergast was old, unwashed, and frog-eyed, with protuberant white-rimmed orbs that stared and stared. But he was a marquis, the same as Uncle's despised brother-in-law. Mr. Martin didn't care that three wives had predeceased Prendergast, nor that the man had gambled away all three of their dowries. That was why, Dree surmised, he was now sniffing around Carrie and her rich portion. His house was ancient and unimproved, sitting in the midst of an undrained swamp. It looked more like something out of a Minerva Press novel than the setting for delicate, sensitive Carinne, who simply did not have the courage to be a heroine. Which was why Carinne was upstairs weeping, and Audrina was about to knock on her uncle's door.

"What is it, girl? Can't you see I'm busy?" Uncle Augustus did not look up from his papers.

Dree smoothed the creases on her gown. She only hoped her cheeks didn't still appear reddened from the cold. "I only need a moment of your time, sir. It's about the house party at Briarwoods."

Augustus looked up from his desk and frowned, whether at her usual unkempt appearance, the interruption, or mention of an event that might entail an outlay of funds on his part, Audrina did not know.

"What is it to you, missy? If you've come to beg for a new gown or some gewgaw, save your breath. Swells like those ain't interested in vicars' daughters. Can't wed 'em or bed 'em, so they don't pay 'em no nevermind, no matter how fancy they're rigged out."

Now her face was red anyway. She could feel the heat in her cheeks. "Of course not, sir. I never thought otherwise. But they might be attracted to a beautiful, well-dowered girl like Carinne."

He raised his voice: "Carinne is as good as spoken for, missy. I told you both, and that's the end of it."

Dree put her hands behind her back so he couldn't see her wringing them. "But the banns have not been read, there's been no formal announcement. Why, Lord Prendergast hasn't even made Carrie an offer."

"That's because the silly twit won't come out of her room to see the man," he shouted. "And I won't have it, do you hear me? That gal is turning into a mealy-mouthed watering pot, just like her mother. And she said she'd feel better if you came to stay. Hah! Much good you've been." He pounded his fist on the desk. "Well, I've about reached the end of my patience with both of you, do you hear me?"

Since the end of her uncle's patience followed hard on the beginning of her uncle's patience, Dree hurried on: "But, sir, nothing has been signed yet and . . . and two of the houseguests are bachelors."

Mr. Martin grunted. He'd heard the news and made his own inquiries. "Podell's here to avoid the bill col-

25

lectors at his door, and Blanford's giving advice about some horses. That's all."

"Oh, but that's not what I heard, sir. Mrs. Dodd's sister said she heard it directly from one of the maids at Briarwoods, that Lady Halbersham was happy as a grig, playing matchmaker."

"Hmm. Podell would be wise to get himself a wife. That's about all the basket-scrambler can do now to get out of dun territory."

Basket-scrambler? The *on dit*, from those who swore they'd seen the baron when he drove through the village on his way to Briarwoods, was that Lord Podell was a veritable Adonis. No one mentioned that he was a profligate. "The other gentleman is an earl," she ventured.

"And as well to pass as t'other is below hatches. Blanford's too proud to trade on his title besides."

"But he hasn't seen Carinne yet!" Audrina was sure no gentleman could resist her exquisite cousin.

"Bah, he's seen all the beauties of London without once throwing the handkerchief. That Podell, now, just might be in the market for a carefully reared wife. No, the flat's only a baron."

"But he's young, Uncle," Audrina almost pleaded. "They both are. Either gentleman is bound to be a better husband for Carinne than Lord Prendergast. She's afraid of him, Uncle, and he smells!" Her own patience was wearing a trifle thin, due mostly to being left standing while her uncle sat behind his desk. She raised her chin. "She's your own daughter, sir. Surely you want her to be happy."

"With a London fribble?" But he was thinking, Dree could tell, about how Halbersham's friends had the entrée everywhere, right up to Carleton House. His daughter would be a fine London lady, instead of being immured in some dank castle with no one to appreciate her elevation in rank except the rats. He rubbed his chin.

26

"The Earl of Blanford is not such a young man. He'll be wanting a son. . . ."

"Stow your blather, girl. Blanford's too downy a cove to be caught by a pretty face. But Podell . . . I wonder how deep in debt the gudgeon is. Baroness, eh? I just might happen to have a word with the chap at the assembly this week. Suppose they'll be there, if he's serious about jumping into parson's mousetrap. Prendergast can wait."

Dree almost collapsed with relief, and from trying to keep her knees from knocking for so long. She felt confident enough to urge her uncle not to speak to Podell. "You'll ruin everything!"

Martin's jaws snapped shut. "What's that, missy?"

Audrina had just saved her cousin from an arranged marriage; she wasn't about to see her thrown into another one, with another fortune hunter. "Why don't you wait until they meet? After all, the earl is still unattached. He might fall in love with Carrie at first sight. Stranger things have been known to happen."

Augustus eyed her through slitted eyes. "What's it to you, missy, eh, pushing this earl on me? I've got it, you think he's the better catch so Carinne will have more pin money to toss to you and that feckless father of yours. Or are you hoping she'll find a place for you in his lordship's London household?"

In her usual honesty, Dree had to admit to herself that she'd always wanted to see London, the sights, the size of it. She'd even hoped once that her uncle would relent and send Carinne there for a Season. Dree would have gone along as her abigail if they'd let her. Now all she wanted was to see her cousin settled with a man who would treat her kindly.

"Whether you believe me or not, Uncle, I only wish Carinne's happiness." And Dree knew Carrie would only find it if her husband wanted *her*, not her dowry. Carrie deserved a love match, not some cold business transaction. She deserved better, and better than a

27

down-at-heels fortune hunter. Dree vowed to herself that, having gone this far, she'd try to win the earl, the hero, the nonpareil, for Carinne. "So I can tell her there is no engagement to Prendergast?"

"Lord and Lady Halbersham are giving a ball for Valentine's Day, eh? There's bound to be socializing sooner than that. I can hold Prendergast off till then without losing him entirely, if you can get Podell to come up to scratch. You'll have to get the chit to stop blubbering, and get her to show some spirit. A man wants a real woman for his wife, not some pretty doll. I'll make sure Podell knows the size of her dot."

Podell might know the size of Carrie's dowry, but Dree meant to make double sure it was the Earl of Blanford who'd collect it.

Chapter Four

*L*ords Blanford and Podell drove to Briarwoods in one day in Max's curricle. Max kept his hat on the entire drive.

The Halbershams came together into the foyer to greet them, with a butler and three footmen to collect their wraps. Max took a deep breath and cursed Thistlewaite to eternal damnation.

"Think of it as a dowager's turban," the valet had suggested. "Or a crown of state." Max thought of it as a small prehistoric rodent that had crawled to his forehead to die, its feet stuck in the tar pits of gum arabic. "You'll grow used to it," Thistlewaite swore. Max never had grown used to the fleas and lice in Spain, so why this vermin should be any different, he couldn't imagine, despite the valet's assurances that it was human hair. A dead human? A beggar selling his filthy mop for a cup of Blue Ruin? Sweepings from a barber's floor? Gads, it boggled the mind. And it itched. No matter, Max misdoubted he'd get used to looking like a billiard ball any time soon either. He took a deep breath and handed over his curly-brimmed beaver.

"Delighted you decided to come," his host said, enthusiastically shaking Max's hand. "Another male, don't you know. House is at sixes and sevens, what with preparations for the ball." He slapped Max's back to emphasize his welcome.

Blanford's fingers twitched, to reach up for reassurance or, barring that, to plant his doltish friend a facer. Instead he turned to his hostess, who was also in a dither, explaining to Franny that there would not be many other guests until the day of the ball, with so much to do. She was staring at Podell as he unwrapped his muffler, then divested himself of his greatcoat. Franny wore a puce waistcoat under a coat of lavender superfine with buttons as big as dinner plates, and a spotted Belcher neckcloth tied loosely around his neck. His blond curls were perfectly in place, even after a day in the carriage with a hat on. Viola clapped her hands. "Oh, they'll just adore you!"

Franny was choking on a reply when Max addressed Viola. He still didn't trust a bow, so he took her hands and raised them to his lips.

Viola batted her eyelashes at him. "Why, Max, maybe there is hope for you after all." Gordie was glaring, so Max told her to save the flirting for her husband, at which she turned her attention back to Franny.

Max had started to breathe again when Gordie asked, "What, parting your hair different, Max?"

They all swiveled to stare at his new thatch. "Thistlewaite got carried away, is all," he said, vowing to see the valet carried away—in a pine box!

Viola was studying him, unsure. "Well, it's vastly becoming," she finally announced. "Let's hope you don't raise too many expectations, Max, if you don't mean to be accommodating."

"Let's hope your new style doesn't become the rage, rather," Gordie put in, "for the sake of us stodgy old unfashionables."

And for the sake of free-ranging rodents everywhere, Max amended. Then the moment was blessedly past. Viola took Franny's arm to lead him down the hall. Max and Gordie followed, grinning at the conversation. "Now, dearest," she was saying, as if she weren't ten years Franny's junior, "you must realize I couldn't invite only the heiresses, of course. I couldn't slight the squire or the other local families. But I have made a list of those females whose acquaintance you should particularly pursue. I mean, it wouldn't do for you to fall top over tree for some pretty chit, now that you've decided to take the plunge, if she cannot relieve your, ah, financial difficulties."

Max could see the perspiration dripping down Franny's neck, the poor sacrificial lamb. No way was Max going to let Lady Vi get a hint of his own intentions, but he just might peruse that list of the vicinity's wellborn females.

At dinner that evening the gentlemen were introduced to the rest of the small house party. Viola's younger brother Warden was there by mischance, having been sent down from school. The lad fancied himself a poet, and wore his hair in long, flowing locks to his shoulders. Max hated him on sight.

There were also two youngish females, bosom bows of Viola's, invited to even out the numbers. The Peckham sisters were a few years past their come-outs, if you counted years in dogs' ages, and they were everything Max didn't want in a wife. Oh, they were pretty enough and well mannered, dressed in the height of London fashion, albeit too gaudy for a simple country dinner. But they also giggled and simpered and lisped, and they fluttered their eyelashes at him so hard, Max feared for his toupee, caught in the crosswind. Their only interests seemed to be in gowns and gossip, with no willingness to be pleased with the usual country pastimes like walking or riding. They did not want to visit the local church or the nearby village, and were bored after one day at Briarwoods, to Viola's chagrin. If they thought Max was going to stay indoors all day entertaining them, they were more corkbrained than they seemed. And if they thought to attach his interest with pouting and striking poses, they were outright attics-to-let. He might offer for a female like that—when hell froze over.

"The pond might be frozen soon. Perhaps we can get up a skating party," Viola offered with a hint of desperation. Then she brightened. "And there is the assembly at Upper Throckton tomorrow night. You'll get to meet my neighbors."

Which was worse, trying to ensnare a gentleman with a lady's looks or with her father's pocketbook? Dree refused to acknowledge that prickling of guilt over what she was doing. She was *not* hoping to snabble an unsuspecting, unwilling *parti* for Carinne; she just wanted to bring her cousin to the attention of the eligibles. Then they could discover Carrie's inner goodness for themselves.

"Perhaps a dab of rouge, Meg?" she asked her cousin's maid, biting her lip.

"Miss Audrina, and you a vicar's daughter! Face paint, indeed!"

"Yes, but my cousin looks as pale as her bedclothes. Carrie, can't you stop fidgeting?"

"How can I when ... when ..."

"When your whole life depends on tonight's assembly? Because of that, peagoose!" Meg was reaching for the hare's-foot brush. "And there is nothing to worry about. You look exquisite, as always." Dree twitched at the tiny puff sleeves of Carrie's pale pink gown, with its overdress of white net strewn with silk roses that matched the flowers woven through Carrie's golden hair. "Like a fairy princess."

"I wish you had a new gown, too, Dree. I could have—"

"No, you do enough. And I couldn't have used my allowance for such frippery, when Papa gives so much of his salary to the needy. What's new finery compared

32

to enough firewood at the vicarage? My ivory gown is good enough."

Carrie looked doubtful and Meg clucked her tongue. The old satin gown hadn't been good enough for the year and a half Dree had been wearing it. It was once Audrina's mother's, and was once white. She'd dyed it with tea, but it was still out of style, ill fitting, and well known at the local assemblies. Audrina fingered the new blue ribbons she'd spent precious pennies on. Sometimes she wished things were different, too, but she wasn't one to lament over what couldn't be changed, so she flashed her cousin her best smile. "What good would a new gown do me anyway, silly, when everyone will be looking at you? You have enough beauty for the family. And no new frock is going to fix this"—she fussed with an errant orangy red curl, already escaping its matching blue ribbon—"or give me your elegant inches so much in style. Or a bosom."

"Dree!"

"Well, it's true, and made you laugh. See, you *can* enjoy yourself. Just think, you're not engaged to old frog-face. That should be enough to celebrate. And if none of the men there tonight pleases you, well, we'll think of something else."

"Like staying in my room so Prendergast couldn't make his offer in form? That was brilliant, Dree!"

"And it got us this time. So do not fret yourself, but *do* try to smile at all the rich, handsome, charming earls you meet. It shouldn't be too difficult. According to Mrs. Harribow at the inn, the gentlemen stopped there on their ride yesterday, and the earl was everything gracious." She didn't say how Mrs. Harribow only wanted to go on and on about the other gentleman, the one with blond hair and heavenly blue eyes, in the most elegant clothes that lady had ever seen. "Not high in the instep at all. And George at the livery said he was mounted on

33

the finest bit of blood and bone in all England, and rode like the wind. 'A regular goer,' " she quoted.

"Oh dear. You know I can't . . . That is, I don't . . . They're so big, Dree." There went all the color from Carrie's cheeks, except the spots brushed on.

Dree cursed herself and patted her cousin's hand. "No gentleman expects a lady to ride neck or nothing, dearest. Just wait till he hears you at the pianoforte. That's what a man admires." She spoke authoritatively, to cover her total lack of knowledge, experience, or conviction. Carrie was trained in all the ladylike pursuits such as watercolors and needlework. They had to be worth something, hadn't they?

Carrie was still worried about the horses, Dree could tell. Her cousin was twisting the strings of her beaded reticule into knots. Dree took the bag from her to untangle. "No matter what else, you can be happy that Lord Prendergast won't be there tonight. He thinks himself above the common folk who can attend if they have the subscription fee."

"I heard he once had to partner the butcher's wife, and that was the last time he came to an assembly." Carrie's smile flickered. "Lord Blanford isn't like that, is he? I mean, he won't expect me to cut my friends dead, will he, like Mama's family did? What if he . . . He might . . ."

He'd better not, Dree swore to herself, but she told her cousin, "Of course not. He wouldn't be coming, else. And you know how the whole town was buzzing when Lady Halbersham reserved all those extra tickets."

"Yes, for those London ladies in her house party. Oh, Dree, I know they'll put us all to shame with their fine manners and clothes and jewels!"

"No one can outshine you," Dree said firmly. "And the *on dit* is that those two friends of Lady Halbersham's are firmly on the shelf. But if they try to capture all the gentlemen's attention, I'll . . . I'll . . ." She was sounding like her cousin now. "I'll spill punch on their gowns so they have to go home."

"Dree, you wouldn't!"

Meg clucked her tongue again. "Miss Audrina, your papa would be shamed, he would."

Papa would already be mortified if he knew his daughter was wondering what it would be like to wear diamonds and pearls and have an elegant gentleman flirt with her. Perhaps some handsome nobleman would ask her to ride? Dree had never been mounted on anything more exciting than her papa's old cob. Perhaps he'd sweep her off her feet and away to London, to countless balls and entertainments. Perhaps he'd offer Papa a fortune, for the honor of his daughter's hand.

Perhaps she'd get so excited if he even noticed her that she'd spill the punch on her own skirts.

Chapter Five

It was just a dance, like countless others the earl had attended, with the same overheated rooms, the same insipid refreshments, the same inane chatter. Unlike most parties Lord Blanford usually graced, here he would be expected to dance with the schoolmaster's sister, the drayman's daughter, and the not-so-prepossessing niece of the neighboring squire. He wouldn't have minded in the ordinary way of things. Didn't he always have a dance with his housekeeper at Public Day fetes? The mixed company reminded Max of his army days, which he hated, except for the men who'd likewise come from all walks of life. None of their sisters was a suitable Countess of Blanford either. And if he did take the floor, Max told himself, good manners dictated that he dance with his hostess and then the Peckham sisters, his fellow houseguests. Duty dances would take half the evening, with no opportunity to look about him for those females on Viola's list. He was determined to find his bride as expeditiously as possible.

What convinced him to look for her along the walls rather than on the dance floor, though, was the music. No graceful waltzes for this company; they were too fast. Instead the small orchestra played country dances, mad jigs and boisterous reels. With all that hopping and capering about in this heat, he'd be wearing his hairpiece as a mustache next.

Max dared not chance it, so he made his excuses as soon as his party was settled in the assembly room. "You'll have to do the honors tonight, Gordie, Frances. You, too, Warden. My apologies, ladies, I can't dance. War wound, don't you know." He limped off, leaving at least one of his friends openmouthed.

"War wound? I thought he caught a fever, not a bu—Ouch!"

Lord Halbersham kicked Franny. "Not the thing to discuss in front of the ladies."

Max found the punch bowl, and a convenient post he could lean against, to watch the company. He made note of the females Lady Halbersham dragged Franny toward between dances, to put his name on their cards. From his vantage point, Max could see that Vi kept trying to head Franny toward two specific females, an absolutely stunning blonde and a little redheaded frump of a thing. The smaller chit kept taking the other's hand and dragging her off, into the arms of the innkeeper, the squire's son, and other local lads. All of the blonde's partners gazed worshipfully at the beauty, while the redheaded girl kept throwing glances in Max's direction, the forward baggage.

The little dowd in the dingy gown wasn't the only female trying to catch his eye, of course, but Max couldn't help watching the two girls, and wondering. One was so elegant, with a dress from one of Bond Street's priciest modistes, if he was any judge, and a diamond necklace that outshone anything in the room. The other was as shabby as the worn-out draperies pulled closed against the night air. She was just as popular as her friend, though, dancing every dance also. The young sprigs she chose as partners didn't just stare into her eyes, either, they laughed and chatted, and skipped merrily along. Max was feeling ancient again. Dash it, he thought, if he hadn't listened to Thistlewaite, he could have been on the dance floor having a high old time, too!

He asked Viola about the two females when the orchestra took a short intermission and his party gathered near the pillar he was supporting.

"The taller one is Miss Carinne Martin. I've been trying to introduce her to Franny all night, but the wretched girl keeps moving around and dancing. Her father is Augustus Martin."

"Of the shipbuilding company?" At Viola's nod, Max whistled. "Not even Franny could run through that fortune."

Viola nodded again. "Exactly. And her father is said to be holding out for a title, so it's perfect. The father is totally unacceptable, of course, but there's good blood on the mother's side. Miss Martin has been carefully raised, educated at a very proper young ladies' seminary in Bath. And she is certainly a beauty. That's why I've been trying to introduce her to Franny all night."

It sounded ideal, for Franny. "And the other?" he heard himself asking. He watched the redhead laughingly accept her blue ribbon from her last partner and try to tie back the wayward curls that tumbled about her shoulders. That fiery mane would look better spread out on a pillow, he found himself thinking.

"That hoyden?" one of the Peckham sisters asked, jealous of his interest. "She's naught but a poor relation, hanging on Miss Martin's sleeve."

Viola had also noticed Max's interest, and she read it correctly. "She might be a poor relation, but it's on the maternal side. One of the Dorset Kennleworths, don't you know. Besides, she's the vicar's daughter, Max, so don't get any untoward notions. You can take that gleam in your eye straight back to your fancy pieces in

London. I'll not have you working your wiles on such an innocent child as Audrina Rowe."

That innocent child was waving her fan at him in unmistakable invitation, unless Max missed his guess. He decided to stroll in that direction. For Franny's sake.

"Come on, old chap. Let's see if we have better luck scraping up an invitation to Miss Martin for you. Wealth and beauty, what more can a fellow ask?"

Conversation, for one. Miss Martin kept her eyes on the floor and her lips firmly closed. Luckily the cousin spoke up as soon as the squire's wife completed the introductions. Unfortunately, the vicar's daughter addressed all of her remarks to Max. Miss Audrina Rowe seemed determined to ignore Franny altogether, quickly asking about Max's journey, his first opinions of the neighborhood, even about his horse.

"For you must know the villagers are singing the praises of your mount. My cousin has a great appreciation of fine horseflesh. She rides out all the time, don't you, Carinne?"

Carinne blanched. She never rode anything but her ancient pony, and then only when no one was about to drive her in the carriage. Franny was squirming. Max crossed his arms over his chest, no help at all.

Audrina was not about to give up. "Do you enjoy music, Lord Blanford? We're thinking of having a musicale. Carinne has the loveliest voice. I swear, she's better than any I've heard." Since Dree had heard no trained voices at all, ever, that was not such a rapper as the horseback riding. Encouraged to be once again on the side of the truth, she rushed on: "And watercolors! How Carinne can paint! I only wish I was artistic, but she must have received all of the talent in the family. Have you viewed Somerset House, Lord Blanford? One of Carinne's instructors had a painting exhibited there. Perhaps you've seen it. What was the man's name, Carrie?"

"Mr. ... Mr. ..." The beauty raised her eyes in agony to her cousin, but caught Lord Podell's admiring gaze instead. Franny smiled.

"Not great on names m'self, Miss Martin."

Carinne smiled back. Dree looked from her beautiful cousin to the beautiful young man in his burgundy velvet coat crisscrossed by fob chains and ribbons. They were gazing at each other like mooncalves. Carrie hadn't spared a glance for Lord Blanford, keeping her eyes firmly on the toes of her shoes. How could Carrie prefer that dandy to the earl in his understated black with white unmentionables? Lord Blanford was elegant, refined, wearing his obviously expensive clothes with unstudied grace, instead of being worn by starched shirt collars and a cravat that could swaddle three infants. Why, the man was a fop, besides being a fortune hunter!

As the music started up again, Dree turned to the earl. "You don't dance, my lord?"

So she'd noticed. Max wasn't surprised. He was used to having females notice his actions. "War wound," was all he said. "Sorry."

"My cousin will be pleased to sit out with you, won't you, Carrie?'"

"But I was ... That is, Mr. Thatcher ..."

"Why, Mr. Thatcher," the minx chirped, "here you are right on time for our dance."

As Max watched, Miss Rowe latched on to a gaptoothed lad in rough clothes who was as coherent as Miss Martin. Max would swear it was the first Mr. Thatcher knew of his promised dance with the little redhead. Before he or Max could protest, though, the chit grabbed the hand of a young female in yellow ruffles and had her partnered to Franny for the *contra danse* forming. They all left, leaving him with the tongue-tied heiress. Max was equally dumbfounded. Dashed if he hadn't been outmaneuvered by a flea-sized nobody as managing as a dowager duchess. But why?

Viola had said the chit was an innocent, but she'd

been casting out lures to him all evening. He'd caught enough in his time to know. The audacious female was a regular flirt who'd make a perfect Cyprian, if she wasn't a vicar's daughter. But why hand him, the biggest fish in the matrimonial waters, over to her cousin? What kind of female would do that? None he knew. Most young ladies he knew, in fact, wouldn't stand next to such a diamond as Miss Martin, much less befriend her. Miss Audrina Rowe was decidedly not an ordinary girl.

Just look at her dance, Max mused, curls tossed every which way, her laughter ringing out when her hair ribbon got lost and trampled. London females would be devastated. They'd be cringing if forced to appear in such an outmoded frock, hiding in the corners so no one saw the darned patches on their gloves. Not Miss Rowe. She was laughing and enjoying herself—and so was her partner. The farm lad had got over his disappointment quickly enough, Max saw, as the boy laughed with her and held her hand longer than the figures of the dance required. Max didn't like him. He was sure that Thatcher chap was a dirty dish. And hadn't there been a whiff of the stables still about him?

The earl's scowl had Carinne cowering at his side, which earned him a fierce look from the cousin, as she and Thatcher turned in the pattern of the dance. Miss Rowe's frown brought Max back to earth, and back to his manners. He was a gentleman, after all.

"Your cousin is an excellent dancer," Max put forth.

His conversational offering was the proper choice, for Miss Martin instantly agreed, without a hint of a stutter, even going so far as to add, "She is the finest cousin a girl could have."

Max's questions about her other relatives, her preferred dance, and comments on the neighboring scenery, anything he could think of, brought back the stammer. It took all of his charm to coax a complete sentence out of the beauty. And then it was: "Oh dear, I wish Dree were here."

"Dree? Miss Audrina?" At her nod he spoke his frustration at finding himself in a backwater with an awkward handful. "She can't always be around to entertain your dance partners, you know."

Those china-doll blue eyes glimmered. Tears? Good grief, Max thought, the chit was going to cry, right there in the assembly rooms. He knew without looking that the cousin would be shooting him dagger looks. Devil take managing females! He renewed his efforts with Miss Martin, fabricating a childhood as a shy, stuttering boy who hated being out among strangers. Miss Martin was actually smiling at his Banbury tale by the time Thatcher brought Miss Rowe back.

Dree flashed the earl a radiant smile to see her cousin looking so comfortable. She was right: they were a perfect pair. Her self-congratulations ended as the earl handed Carinne to Lord Podell for the next dance. There was no way Dree could prevent that dance, not without causing a scene that might give the earl a disgust of them altogether. Her smile faded even more when Lord Blanford turned to her again.

"Perhaps you'll take pity and sit out this set with a poor veteran, Miss Rowe, while your cousin does my friend the honor of dancing?" Max tried not to smirk, wondering how Miss Rowe appreciated being outflanked.

She didn't like it at all. "It's a pity indeed about your injury. How fortunate it doesn't interfere with your neck-or-nothing riding."

Max only smiled at the sarcasm, trying to remember to limp when he brought her a lemonade. She glared at him over the cup. What had the volatile chit in the boughs now? he wondered. She had the most eligible man in the room fetching her drink, and all she could do was glower. Her ill temper wasn't directed at him, Max belatedly realized, but at her peahen of a cousin

42

who was gliding serenely on Franny's arm, smiling into the eyes of her handsome partner without a hint of awkwardness. Franny was grinning back, relieved he didn't have to make conversation. Together they were a fairytale couple, and Miss Rowe was acting the evil stepsister.

"Bedfordshire is surprisingly full of charming young ladies," Max ventured, although why he thought to turn the vixen up sweet, he didn't know, except for a wish to see that carefree delight she'd shown the farmer.

Lukewarm and trite as it was, Max's compliment did restore Audrina's good humor. He'd been caught! Dree had to clutch her hands together to keep from clapping. "My cousin, you mean. Isn't Carrie the most beautiful girl in the world? And she's as good and kind as she is pretty. I just knew you'd like her if you got the chance to know her."

And Miss Rowe went on extolling her cousin's talents and traits, with a dazzling smile lighting up her face. The freckles that would sink a London deb's chances seemed to belong with that radiant glow, Max thought, like sunshine. She even had dimples. Max listened to her happy babble with half an ear while he admired the view, until her words and intent finally sunk in. Miss Audrina Rowe was matchmaking on her beautiful, wealthy cousin's behalf! He was astounded again at her unselfishness, and then he was chagrined. The vicar's daughter, a frumpy, flyaway little female, wasn't interested in the Earl of Blanford—except as a *parti* for her relation! And for this he was wearing the clippings from a shorn poodle?

Chapter Six

Gordon, Lord Halbersham, wasn't having any better time of it. He took up a position near Max's pillar after Miss Rowe skipped away on the arm of another bucolic beau. From there the viscount could watch his wife flirt with every man in the room from the septuagenarian squire to some spotted youth. Whilst Gordie listened to Viola tittering at some remark from an ill-clad country-man, Max listened to Gordie's teeth grinding. Fine, Max thought, he'd lose his hair; Gordie'd lose his choppers.

"Deuce take it, man, don't just stand there. Take the chit home and make her forget that any other man exists on this earth."

"You mean . . . ?"

"Yes, you clothhead, that's precisely what I mean. Go now before you can only gum at her earlobes. You can send the carriage back for Franny and me. We'll see the Peckham sisters home."

"What will I tell Viola to get her to leave so early?"

"You're the diplomat, Gordie. You can think of some reason. Or tell her you have the headache. Women use that excuse all the time."

"Only because they can't claim war wounds," Gordie

said with a wink as he moved off to cross the dance floor. He tapped his wife's partner on the shoulder and whispered something in Viola's ear that brought an instant blush to her cheeks. Max shook his head. For a politician, Halbersham had no subtlety. But Vi did agree to leave, so perhaps Gordon knew best after all. Who was Max to give advice about women, after tonight's fiasco?

Without Viola to choose his partners, Lord Podell was soon sharing Max's post instead of Halbersham. Together they watched the rest of the assembly.

"Did you meet all the females on Vi's list?" Max asked.

"Enough," Franny replied, grinning hugely. "Ain't she exquisite?"

There was no need to ask which *she* Franny meant. "A diamond of the first water indeed, but—"

"No buts. She's the one."

"How can you be sure? It's early days, man. You've only had one dance with the chit, and not a lot of conversation at that, I'd guess." He'd swear, in fact, that Miss Martin didn't have two bits of conversation to rub together.

Franny rocked on his heels, looking like the cat that got the canary. "A chap just knows. Miss Carinne is quiet, peaceful-like. She came right out and told me she didn't expect a fellow to keep thinking up things to say. You know, that humgudgeon the poetic types are always spouting at a pretty gal. Embarrass her, she said. Would embarrass me to say it. We suit."

"I still say it's early days to be calling the banns. You haven't met her father yet. I hear he's a rum go."

"According to Viola, all he cares about is snabbling a title and getting his daughter accepted in London society. You know I've got the entrée everywhere."

Max thought of that tongue-tied chit in the midst of Almack's patronesses. Might as well feed her to the lions at the Tower. "Do you think Miss Martin would like London? You said yourself she's quiet."

"And you said I should marry a rich girl and install her at m'country place. But I've half a mind to take Miss Martin to London anyway. Show her off, don't you know. She'll like the shops and the theater. And if she don't talk to anyone else, well, at least I won't have to worry myself to flinders like poor Gordon." Franny twirled his quizzing glass on its ribbon, satisfied. Then he raised it to his eye to examine Max more closely. "I say, you ain't trying to discourage me because you're interested yourself, are you? Beautiful girl and an heiress. I couldn't blame you."

"No, no, I've no intention of trying to cut you out with Miss Martin. I just think you should get to know her better before making such a momentous decision."

Franny didn't hear anything but the denial. "Good. Her father'd toss me on my ear if he thought you were in the running. Stands to reason. Any father would. Mean to say, don't have much to offer. But I'll swear to make her happy. Mean it, too. That should win him over."

Not from what Max had heard about Augustus Martin. "Lud, just don't go plead your case too soon or he'll think you're a Bedlamite, or a fortune hunter. Once you get to know the chit, then you can swear undying devotion, not yet."

Franny sucked on the handle of the looking glass. "How long? Mean to say, all these other chaps won't let such a jewel go unclaimed. Do you think a week's enough time to convince Mr. Martin I'm sincere about Miss Carinne?"

"Wait a month at least. Then, once you know her better, you can put your luck to the test if you're of the same mind."

"Two weeks. And I will be."

* * *

Audrina was right: the party from Briarwoods did not attend services at her father's church the next morning, but not because the Halbershams felt themselves too grand for the humble village chapel. They overslept. Then they had to bundle their guests into carriages for the ride to Upper Throckton for the late service. After church the viscount and his lady disappeared upstairs again, which had the Peckham sisters tittering and Viola's brother Warden snickering over his mutton until Max fixed him with a stare.

"You'll have to take over as host for your brother-in-law this afternoon. Lord Podell and I have to make a call at Mr. Martin's White Oaks."

Franny had still felt the same the next morning. He was all for riding out to visit, to see if Miss Martin could be as lovely by daylight, until Max reminded him it was Sunday. He would have to wait till late afternoon, at least.

"You'll come along, won't you, Max? Mean to say, you know how to go on."

Max rather thought he would accompany Franny, and not only to oversee the other's courtship. Warden thought he might accompany them, too. "What, and leave our two charming fellow guests alone?"

Warden groaned. His Greek studies weren't half as boring as those two haughty Peckham females. "But I'd like to quiz Miss Rowe about her knowledge of the classics. With her father the vicar, and him giving lessons, perhaps she'd—"

"No," Max snapped. Warden had youth and hair. He didn't need the company of the only interesting female in the neighborhood.

The interesting female was shredding a roll. Uncle Augustus was taking his midday meal with associates in Throckton, so the two cousins had the dining room to themselves. Carinne wasn't eating her nuncheon either, but instead of fretting, Miss Martin was staring dreamily into space, her lips gently curved. Almost like an angel getting her first glimpse of heaven, Dree thought impatiently. "What do you mean, you prefer Lord Podell? I grant you, the man is as handsome as a Greek god, but truly, Carrie, how can you? He's naught but a man-milliner."

"So elegant, such a sense of style. And kind."

"Kind? The man is a fortune hunter! Why, you'd never know if he cared for you or for your father's gold."

"I'd never know with any man, but Lord Podell seemed to like me."

"Perhaps he was just being polite. We might never see any of the Briarwoods party again. They didn't attend church." And Carinne could be awkward at times, Dree had to admit. Such a distinguished gentleman as the Earl of Blanford was used to more sophisticated company.

"He'll come." Carinne was positive. And pleased.

"But a Bond Street strutter, Carrie? You know you never wanted to go to London."

"I never wanted a Season, rather. I'd enjoy the shops and seeing the sights. And you were the one who tried to convince me to go, for the cultural advantages. Besides, Lord Podell means to make his property in Warwick his home for most of the year."

"What, that starched and curled dandy means to set up as a farmer?"

"He intends to try to bring his estates back into prosperity."

"He means to reclaim his acreage with your money, you mean."

"I'd rather that than see Lord Prendergast gamble it all away, wouldn't you?"

"Anything is better than Lord Prendergast," Audrina conceded, finally taking a bite of her capon. She waited till the footman brought the dessert pudding before she tried again. "Don't you think you might consider Lord

Blanford?" She pictured the earl, tall and broad, with an air of command about him. He was strong, confident, capable. In short, everything manly. Dree knew her own experience of men was woefully short, but didn't doubt for a minute that his lordship would stand out in any gathering, noblemen or otherwise. "He's quick-witted and amusing, too."

"He frightens me."

"Spiders frighten you, goose. Do say you'll try to be friendly, if he should pay his addresses."

Carinne dropped her spoon. "Oh, I pray he won't! Papa will be sure to prefer him to Lord Podell."

And for once Audrina would agree with Uncle Augustus, but she'd keep her own counsel for now.

Miss Rowe might have kept a silent tongue in her mouth, but her actions spoke volumes—to Lord Blanford, at least—when he and Franny were shown into the ornately furnished drawing room that afternoon. Audrina jumped up and rang for tea after the initial greetings, and then tugged at Lord Podell's arm until he joined her on the crocodile-legged sofa, leaving Max to sit next to Miss Martin on the facing couch.

The others were oblivious to the machinations, however. After examining his saffron satin sleeve for hints of creases, Franny stared across the space into Miss Martin's eyes. She stared back, a tinge of rose on her creamy cheeks. The two could have been alone on the moon for all the attention they paid Dree and the earl. And they did look wondrous together, Dree had to admit, his lordship like a jonquil, and Carrie in a pale rose muslin that showed off her rounded form and elegant shoulders. A veritable garden of beauty.

Audrina frowned. Max grinned, as though he could read her thoughts, earning him another fierce look for not trying harder to engage her cousin in conversation. Dree couldn't fault the earl's appearance, in navy blue superfine and dove gray pantaloons. That was how a man ought to dress, she firmly believed. How could

Carrie not even glance in his direction? It was all Dree could do to keep from staring at the earl's firm legs, so well fitted were his trousers. And that devilish grin, lop-sided and boyish, with warm brown eyes that had a definite twinkle; how could Carrie ignore him?

It never once occurred to Dree that Lord Blanford was ignoring Carrie. Oh, he'd noticed how stunning she looked in the fashionable high-waisted gown with trailing ribbons—hell, a man would have to be turned to stone not to notice, not to appreciate. But he had a whole collection of beautiful artworks to admire. That wasn't what he wanted in a wife. Of course, a hobble-dehoy schoolgirl like Miss Rowe, in a shapeless sack of indeterminate color after so many washings and turnings, wasn't what he wanted either. The chit's red hair was all atumble again, and no, his fingers were not itching to feel the silky fire; he only wanted to brush the curls off her satiny cheeks. Freckled cheeks, he amended. The chit had freckles. And she was devious and manipulative, everything he hated in a female. Wasn't she trying to hint Franny away with mention of her uncle's business connections, when asked Mr. Martin's whereabouts? She managed to interject her uncle's sharp dealing, in case he missed the point that the man was in trade.

The only thing Franny missed was the opportunity to meet his future father-in-law and lay his heart at the man's feet. Miss Martin was an angel. Their fingers brushed over the tray of poppy-seed cakes. His day was complete.

Not so Audrina's. She was not ready to give up, even against admittedly overwhelming odds. "We're planning a skating party for the next nice afternoon," she decided that instant. "There's a lovely pond behind the house that the gardeners have cleared of last week's snow. They say it is well frozen. We'll have a bonfire going alongside, and Cook can provide hot cider. We were hoping you would come, with the rest of Lady Halbersham's house party, of course."

What Dree was hoping, of course, was that Lord Podell would refuse. The popinjay wouldn't want to get his clothes mussed, she thought. Or he'd make a cake of himself on the ice, letting the earl's undoubtedly athletic prowess shine.

"Carrie's the most graceful skater in the village," she added for Blanford's sake when he accepted on the house party's behalf, and this time she told the truth. Carrie loved to skate and looked beautiful doing it. Surely the earl could not help but be entranced. And surely Carrie would finally see the overdressed Tulip Podell for a useless ornament.

Of course, Dree hadn't counted on the recent Frost Fair in London, when Lord Podell skated up and down the Thames for days. And she hadn't counted on Lord Blanford's war injury, which was going to keep him off the ice and away from Carinne.

Chapter Seven

$\mathcal{A}$ war injury? If that was what kept the Earl of Blanford at the side of the pond when all the others were gaily skating, how was he to explain to a neighbor lad eager for battle stories? That an enemy saber took off the top of his head and he had to keep a small bearskin rug on it to keep his gray matter warm? That a cannon blast split his skull, so he couldn't bend over for fear of his brains spilling out?

He refused to lie about a shattered knee or such. That would dishonor the wounds his fellow soldiers suffered. He also refused to chance a fall on the ice. There hadn't been much opportunity for practice on the Peninsula, so Max was certain to go down at least once. He didn't mind looking like a jackanapes in front of his friends and their friends by losing his balance, or even losing his hat. His topknot was another story.

Hell and damnation, Max swore as he stomped around the edge of the pond in an effort to keep his toes from freezing, and to keep out of the reach of army-mad youths. What a cursed nuisance. He never should have come into the country where a man was expected to exert himself. He never should have let his valet convince him to don such an unreliable subterfuge. Just last night he'd feared he was going deaf in his dotage, besides, until he realized the blasted thing had slipped sideways, over his ear. Now he was forced to sit on the sidelines, weak-kneed. This was the first time Maxim Blanding had measured his courage and found it wanting. He was also wanting something stronger than the hot mulled cider the Martin servants were pouring out near the bonfire.

And, he had to admit, he was wanting to be out on the ice joining in the fun with an insufferable little female who was spinning madly, playing crack the whip with Warden and some of the local boys. He could pick her out by the red cape she wore—a hand-me-down, he supposed, which clashed horribly with her curls—or by her laughter that rang out even from the pond's farthest shores.

As Max watched, Audrina challenged the boys to a race, tearing across the ice in a mad scramble, all of them bareheaded, the harum-scarum lot. They didn't care if they fell or bumped into anyone, chancing some innocent skater's collapse. Max unconsciously tugged his beaver hat down tighter. He dragged his thoughts away from the hoyden in red before he did something foolish, and his eyes away from the childish fun, before they turned green with envy.

The cousin and Franny skated by, waving to him. Carinne was as graceful as promised, and stunning with her golden beauty framed by the sable lining of the hood of her maroon cape. Franny had a matching maroon muffler tied around his neck, as though they had planned it. Perhaps they had, for Franny hadn't left Miss Martin's side since helping tie on her skates. He even managed to guide their path around obstacles, all the while gazing into the Incomparable's eyes. They skated together as if they'd been doing it for years, and as if to violin music only they could hear. They glided effortlessly into magical turns, in perfect time.

Viola and Gordie were a perfect contrast. They darted

past in fits and starts, chuckling over mishaps, his hat gone flying, her muff skidding across the ice. But they were together, and laughing, Max was glad to see.

Even Mr. Martin made an appearance on the ice. Max thought he must have come to get a look at his prospective son-in-law, but the shipbuilder did lead both Peckham sisters across the frozen pond. He skated in slow, jerky steps, but at least their host was doing his duty by them . . . as Max wasn't.

So he was being discourteous, dishonorable, and deceitful, besides being depressed that he was missing what looked like a fine time. And all for the sake of a few strands of hair. No, a few strands were all he had left on the top. He was putting himself through this torture for his valet's sake. That and his vanity. He was almost of a mind to return to Briarwoods, give Thistlewaite the sack—and the hairpiece—then ride to London to face his future as a doomed, bare-domed bachelor. He'd leave this minute, damned if he wouldn't, before the hair on his chest froze off, too.

Then Miss Rowe skated to a stop in front of him. Her nose was red, adding to the offending color scheme. Max thought she looked adorable.

"I'm sorry about your wound, my lord. I should have thought of some other entertainment that you could enjoy with us."

"No, no. Not at all. I'm quite happy to watch. Very pleasant." Gads, her guilty apology was all he needed to make him feel even lower than the dirt beneath his feet—if he could still feel his feet. To change the subject, Max gestured toward Franny and Carinne, executing intricate figures in the middle of the pond. "They skate magnificently together, don't they?"

"They look like an artist's portrayal of winter bliss," Dree said with a sigh.

"And you don't approve?"

"Forgive me for speaking ill of your friend, but he's

a ne'er-do-well! I didn't want a basket-scrambler for Carrie. She deserves so much better!"

"Have you thought that Franny might see all of her fine qualities, too? Perhaps he likes her, the same as you do."

"He's not worthy of her!"

"Why, because his pockets are to let? It's not his fault, Miss Rowe, that his father gambled away his inheritance and left him with a mound of debts and a mortgaged estate. He's done his best to hold on to Podell Hall for his descendants. And you shouldn't fault a man for the cut of his coat." Or the length of his hair. "Franny can't participate in all the expensive pastimes of his cronies, so he indulges in his tailoring. He's entitled to some pleasure, isn't he?"

"I suppose I've judged him too harshly," Audrina conceded. "But a man's character doesn't show at first; his peacock's costume does."

"I can swear to his character, Miss Rowe. Frances Podell is a good friend, brave and loyal. He's not a gambler or a womanizer. He's just a terrible dresser."

"Carrie thinks he's elegant." Audrina shrugged. "At least he's better than Prendergast."

"Good grief, even a loveless marriage to Franny would be better than that. And I guarantee this isn't merely a match of convenience. Just look at them. You'd have to be blind not to see they are well suited."

Dree didn't have to look. She knew what she'd see: February lovebirds smelling of April and May. And she couldn't look over at the couple ice-dancing on clouds behind her, for she was too busy gathering a handful of the remains of last week's snowfall. She launched her hurriedly rounded missile with deadly accuracy at his lordship's high-crowned beaver hat. "It's too lovely a day to be so stuffy."

His lordship was not amused. He turned and dived after the hat—and his escaping hairpiece—while Dree was still giggling. Max slammed the hat back on before anyone could see what was inside it, instead of being on his head. He was sputtering with anger. Thistlewaite wasn't there for him to strangle, so he took his rage out on Audrina. "You . . . you brat! How dare you? Go play with the other children."

That hurt. Dree had been running her father's household for years, and taking on responsibilities for the parish long before most girls put their skirts down. She knew the earl could never see her as an equal, no matter how pleasantly he acted toward her, since their worlds were so far apart. Yet she thought they might be friends. She'd only meant to bring him some fun, not remind him she was naught but a vicar's ragtag brat.

The others were taking up the game, the men tossing snowballs while the ladies squealed. Lady Halbersham snuck up behind her husband, who was aiming at Franny, and dumped a handful of snow down his collar. Lord Halbersham turned with a roar and scooped his wife up, to deposit her facedown in the bank of cleared snow at the edge of the pond.

Lord Blanford stalked off.

"Starched-up old sobersides," Dree muttered, brushing snowy mittens across suddenly damp eyes. "Lord Frances is a better choice for Carrie after all," she sniffed. "I'm glad she didn't pick any toplofty earl who is too full of himself and his dignity to have a good time. Go play with the children indeed." She couldn't resist one last toss, which landed squarely in the middle of Blanford's broad back. "And don't forget to limp this time," she shouted after him.

The next morning the earl sent a box of bonbons for Audrina, and she made her prettiest apology when he came to call with Franny that afternoon.

"Let's forget the unfortunate episode, shall we?" Max offered. "We mustn't be at odds, for it looks as if we'll be seeing a great deal of each other."

Carinne and Lord Podell were going through music at

the pianoforte, with more glances into each other's eyes than glances at the titles on the sheets. To give them some privacy while still protecting Carinne's reputation, Dree had to lead the earl aside and keep him entertained. She tried to be her most mature and demure, pouring out the tea with the airs of a duchess. Her good intentions lasted until the next morning when the gentlemen arrived with two mares in tow, begging the honor of a ride.

Carinne could do just fine at a walk, Lord Podell assured her. He wouldn't leave her side, the mare was perfectly behaved, and Miss Martin was exquisite in her sapphire blue riding habit.

Audrina was dowdier than ever in her cut-down, threadbare, washed-out brown relic of a riding outfit. It didn't matter. She threw her arms around the dainty mare, then almost embraced the earl in her delight. Instead of that outré behavior, she mounted and set off at a gallop, her bright curls streaming behind her. Max let her lead him and his stallion on a bruising ride through woods and over streams, content to listen to her merry laughter. The others could have been in the next county for all they knew or cared.

After that they rode out or drove—for Carinne's sake—every nice day, sometimes taking the rest of the Halbershams' guests along sightseeing, where Audrina's knowledge of the old abbeys and Roman fortresses impressed even young Warden. In the evenings they all often met at one neighbor's or another's for cards, music, charades, or dancing.

Carinne was in alt, floating on Lord Podell's arm. Audrina was resigned to the match, convinced it was more than cream-pot affection. And Uncle Augustus was so puffed up with success, he even gave Audrina a twenty-pound bonus, for matchmaking. The solicitors were already meeting, and the engagement would be announced at Lady Halbersham's Valentine's Day ball, two days hence.

"So buy yourself some gewgaw or other, missy. Maybe you can hook one of the blacksmith's boys."

With twenty pounds her papa could feed a lot of poor mouths. And she didn't *want* any of Jed Smith's hairy, dirty, illiterate sons. But Dree folded the note and smiled at her uncle.

"You'd do well to think on it, gal, for that's the last you'll have of me. My girl gets married and moves off, I'll not support you and that nodcock father of yours. Foxed yourself, you did, cutting out old Prendergast. If the chit had wed him, you could have moved in there and still been near your da. Old Prendergast would never have noticed. Now? My Lord and Lady Podell are going on a long bride trip to introduce Carinne to his fancy relatives. He'll see she makes her bows to royalty in the spring, too, see if he don't. I promised him another pile of blunt if it's done right. That leaves you out in the cold, missy."

Audrina straightened her back. "Carrie has invited me to London when they get there."

"What, you'd play dogsberry to a pair of newly-weds?" he goaded.

"And they do intend to settle at Podell Hall," she went on as if he hadn't spoken, or hadn't said anything she hadn't thought of for herself.

"After the place is renovated. My wedding present, don't you know. But aye, I suppose they'll be needing you when they start filling the nursery. Someone has to look after the brats, I suppose. Can't expect my daughter, the baroness, to change nappies. She'll be too busy entertaining the nobs at house parties and such. You still pleased with the match?"

"Carrie's happiness is the only thing that matters."

He snorted. "That and getting a grandson who'll be a baron. I hope that deuced caper-merchant Podell don't take as long about begetting me an heir as he does tying his neckcloths."

Chapter Eight

She could be a governess, Dree thought as she trudged back from the vicarage after giving her father ten of Uncle Augustus's pounds. Or a companion. Either would be preferable to being the perpetual poor relation. Dear Carrie would never make her feel like a drudge, but Audrina was well aware that Lord Podell was already wishing her to the devil. Of course, he wanted privacy with his new betrothed; of course, Uncle Augustus ordered her to cling to them like sticking plaster. The only time Dree felt comfortable these days was when Lord Blanford was around. The earl was good company when he came down off his high horse.

Dree kicked a rock in her path. Who was she fooling? The earl wasn't a pleasant companion in her chaperoning duties. He was the most fascinating man she'd ever met, or was ever likely to. And he'd be leaving right after the Valentine's Day ball. He'd most likely come back for the wedding, but for his friend's sake, not hers. Then Carrie would ride off with her fair Lochinvar—and Dree would have to make some kind of life for herself.

Her future looked as bleak as this midwinter day. She supposed she could take Uncle Augustus's advice and find a husband. The Widower Allison needed a mother for his three young children. Tom Rush needed help in his butcher shop. Buck Sharfe needed strong sons to help work his farm. Without a dowry, without a Season in London or even Bath, that was the best she could hope for. But Papa needed the money her employment would bring, and Dree had needs of her own. She saw the stars in Carrie's eyes and wished for a love match, too. Besides, after knowing the Earl of Blanford, a lesser man just wouldn't do. And they were all lesser men, she feared, every male in the kingdom.

Audrina pulled her red cape closer, trying to warm the chill in her heart. How foolish, she chided herself, wishing for what she didn't have. What she did have, the saints be praised, was ten pounds, and the chance to attend her very first fancy ball. She turned her steps toward the little dry goods shop in the village. For once in her life Audrina Rowe was going to look like a lady.

There were bound to be strangers at Lady Halbersham's do, perhaps a gentleman so strange he wouldn't notice he was partnering an impoverished vicar's daughter with fly-away red hair and managing ways. Perhaps he wouldn't mind that Papa's learning was her only dowry, and that her highborn relatives didn't acknowledge her. And perhaps, just perhaps, he wouldn't be a stranger after all.

Velvet as soft as kitten fur, the palest pink of sunset's reflection, that's what Audrina chose, and green ribbons for trim, to match her eyes. With the help of Carinne and her maid, she fashioned a simple gown with tiny puffed sleeves and a skirt that fell straight from the high waist just under her bosom. There were no flounces or lace overskirts or intricate embroidery—there was no time. There were brand-new white gloves, though, and silk stockings. And powder covering most of her freckles, and her hair done up in an intricate braid coiled atop her head, with just a few curls allowed to trail down her shoulder. The maid had pulled Dree's hair so tight, and set in so many hairpins, the arrangement wouldn't dare come undone.

Dree felt almost pretty, until she saw her cousin. Carinne looked like a princess in her silver sarcenet, with the diamond tiara her father presented her as an engagement present. She seemed even happier with the bouquet of flowers Lord Podell had delivered, and instantly demanded the maid weave them through the headpiece. Dree cut some ferns from the potted plant in the hallway and wove them into a wreath for her own hair, so it might look like someone sent her a posy, too.

There, Dree thought as she gathered her lamentably red cape, she'd done her best. It wouldn't be good enough for him, of course, who was so proud and proper, elegant and *à la mode*, but not even the Earl of Blanford could accuse her of looking like the parish brat tonight. That would have to be sufficient. She wasn't fool enough to hope for the sun and the moon.

Downstairs, however, a package waited for her, a nosegay of white rosebuds. The card read: *The supper dance? MB*. If not the sun and the moon, maybe she could hope for a few stars. There were certainly stars in her eyes as she dashed back up the stairs to pin the flowers to the neckline of her gown. Perfect! Except . . . except there was still something missing in her efforts to appear a mature, alluring woman: a bosom. Quickly Dree rolled up a pair of stockings and tucked them in the narrow bodice. *Now* she was ready.

The Earl of Blanford was torn. She was too young, too innocent. He was too old, too battle-scarred by life. But what future did she have without him? Not many men could afford to marry without a dowry; not many would look past the unfashionable clothes to see the charming young woman. The talk was of some menial position, or marriage to some local lout. Marriage to an old, tired rake had to be better.

And what future did he have without her? A cold

one. Oh, he'd find a willing bride, a proper female who didn't like the wind in her hair and who didn't laugh out loud, or tease. She'd give him sons, but she wouldn't give him sunshine.

By Satan's smallclothes, he wasn't that blasted old!

And Miss Audrina Rowe wasn't anyone's little charity-case cousin, not tonight. She was dazzling! Max had to remind himself to shut his mouth. Why, in London she'd be called a Pocket Venus. She'd be a Toast, with her lively sparkle and intelligent conversation. He watched as she left Lady Halbersham's receiving line and entered the pink-draped ballroom through an archway of trailing vines and silk roses designed to look like a heart. For a moment she stood there, the perfect living valentine. She was searching the room—Max could only hope she looked for him—before flocks of men swooped down on her, and not just the neighborhood youngsters. Of course, every libertine in the place would notice her, now that her light wasn't hidden under a bushel of rags from the dustbin. And now that the local beauty was spoken for, albeit the engagement was not yet announced, Miss Rowe was even more in demand.

The earl considered keeping his distance, letting the young men discover her charms, letting one of them fall top over trees in love with his fairy sprite. Then Max wouldn't have to worry about her future or if he should have a place in it.

Such noble restraint lasted halfway into the party. Viola had arranged a lottery for the first dance, with various-colored hearts, cupids, and arrows cut in halves with the parts put into a top hat or a straw bonnet. The ladies and gentlemen each chose one, then had to find their partners by matching halves. Max could have rigged it. He thought about it, about having another dance with her, but he decided not, for then Vi would insist he take the floor with every wallflower in the room. So he stayed on the sidelines, watching Audrina twirl and laugh and charm the pants off every partner she had. In their dreams, at least.

Max was tempted to call out one young buck who never raised his eyes off that bouquet of flowers nestled between her breasts. *My* flowers, Max growled to himself. One dastard kept plying her with champagne. Most likely the chit had never had any before; she should have had her first taste with him. Her next partner held her hand too long, drooling over her glove. That was it! The earl had had enough.

"My dance, I believe, Miss Rowe."

Dree stared up at the earl, taking in his elegant black and white formal attire, the ruby that glowed in his neckcloth, the commanding look on his chiseled countenance. She could have stared all night, if one of her beaus hadn't coughed. She fumbled for the dance card at her wrist. "Oh, but I thought we were to have the supper dance."

"That, too."

Dree was confused, but maybe that was the champagne. "But you don't dance," she insisted.

He held his gloved hand out. "It's Valentine's Day. Everyone dances."

"Oh." She took his hand, took two steps forward, then stopped. "They're playing a waltz."

"Vi thought it was too daring for a country ball, but I bribed the orchestra."

A waltz! Dree might have thought she'd died and gone to heaven, except ... "I don't know how, my lord."

He just smiled. "I do. I'll show you. Just relax."

In his arms? Mere inches from the masculine scent of him, spices and lemons and ... Dree shut her eyes, but the whole room started spinning. She giggled.

"You're foxed, minx. No more champagne for you. Now, listen to the count and let me guide your steps."

She did, and soon found herself floating on the strains of the music, in his embrace. Truly this was the most glorious night of her life, she thought. It was going to be over all too soon, of course, but at least she would have this memory.

At the end of the music, she curtsied, he bowed, and they separated without saying a word.

Letting Audrina go off with her next partner was the hardest thing Max had ever done. Avoiding Viola and her platter-faced misses for the next half hour was almost as difficult.

Then came the supper dance. And it was a rollicking country air, because Vi had threatened to dismiss the orchestra if they played another waltz. Max had always intended to ask Audrina to sit out with him, to take a stroll away from the stifling ballroom toward the hallway and the empty room whose key he held. Unfortunately he'd shown he could dance, without a hint of a limp.

"But it's Valentine's Day," she reminded him. "Everyone dances. Please?"

Oh Lud. He knew she loved to dance. He did, too, for that matter. And he desperately wanted to hold her again, even if merely to twirl her lithe young body in the figures of the dance. He reached up and patted his pate. No slippage. If he was ready to put his fate to the test, he may as well go all the way. Hell, if he was too old to dance with her, he was surely too old to wed with her!

Everyone in their set was laughing and hopping about, dancing with joyous abandon, even the Earl of Blanding. In the face of Audrina's pleasure, he was able to forget his own worries. Then disaster struck.

It was a calamity so unexpected, so catastrophic, that for a moment all of Max's battle-hardened responses fled. He stood stock-still, staring, as a stocking popped out of his partner's bodice, sailed through the air, and unrolled itself at his feet. He shouldn't laugh. Oh Lud, he couldn't laugh, not once Max saw the stricken look on Audrina's face. He'd seen less pitiable expressions on trapped hares. Gathering his wits, he scooped the silk garment into his fist, having pretended to stumble in the dance steps. He whisked the stocking into his pocket and gave Audrina a wink.

She was still standing rigidly, though, color by turns flooding her cheeks and draining away to leave a few freckles in stark relief. Max had seen enough panicked raw recruits to know she wasn't going to budge, not in her mortification. The other couples in their set were already starting to lose their places in the figures, bumping into each other. It was only a matter of time before someone noticed that Miss Rowe wasn't moving, that she was, in fact, listing to starboard as it were. The poor puss couldn't replace the stocking here, nor could she remove the other one with all eyes turning in her direction.

With cries of "For the honor of the regiment" echoing in his mind, Max did the only thing possible. He snatched off his hairpiece, tossed it toward a row of dozing dowagers, and yelled, "Rat! Rat!"

Chapter Nine

$\mathcal{V}$iola Halbersham was never going to forgive him. She might even urge Gordie to call him out for ruining her party—if Gordie stopped laughing long enough to issue a challenge. No matter, Max thought, it was worth it. In the ensuing pandemonium, he'd been able to tug Audrina out of the ballroom with no one giving her a second glance. Everyone was too busy rushing for the exits or tending to swooning ladies.

Max bustled Dree into a small room and locked the door behind him, blocking out the screams and shouts in the hallway. Dree turned her back to him, her shoulders shaking.

"Ah, sweetheart, it's not worth crying about. No one saw."

But she wasn't crying, he saw as she turned to him, the second stocking in her hand. She was laughing and pointing at his bald head!

"I should have left you out there, brat!" But he looked down at the stocking, and had to laugh, too. "The look on your face . . ."

"And yours!" She gasped and wiped tears out of her eyes. "You did *that*, for me?"

Max stopped laughing. "I'd do anything for you, Miss Audrina Rowe."

Then she was in his arms. No, Max told himself, it was only gratitude. Besides, she was too small. He'd get a crick in his neck. But Miss Rowe must have stood on tiptoe, and raised her face along with her arms, pulling his mouth down to hers, for now she felt just right. He was tasting the champagne on her soft, willing lips, and feeling her sweet body pressed against his. And that felt just right, too.

Alas, Max was a gentleman. He set her a bit apart. "Do you mind?"

"Mind? It was the most beautiful kiss I could ever imagine!"

"Not the kiss, sweetheart. Do you mind, you know, about my hair?"

"Mind what?"

"Deuce take it, that I am going bald!"

There, he'd said it. Max half expected her to burst into giggles again, but Dree wasn't laughing. Suddenly shy, she took a step farther away. "It's not for me to mind one way or another, my lord."

"My name is Max, and blast it, of course it is. I know I'm making mice feet of this—I've never done it before, you know—but I am asking you to be my wife."

"Your wife?" Audrina couldn't believe her ears. Her imagination must be running away with her again.

Not precisely thrilled with her reaction, Max repeated, "My wife. Will you do me the great honor of bestowing your hand in marriage?"

"But, but, I'm only a vicar's brat, remember?"

"No, you're everything I want in a wife."

"But I'll never be a grand lady. I'll never know how to go on in your world. Why, look what happened at my very first ball."

"London will adore you, as I do."

Dree could only sigh and say, "Oh, Max." This was what she wanted more than anything in the world, but she knew in her heart she wasn't worthy of him. She twisted the stocking she still held in her hand. "You deserve so much better."

Max took her hesitancy for rejection. "It's me. I'm too old for you. I should have realized."

"Never! Why, someone would think you were in your dotage, to hear you speak, or that I was still in the schoolroom. You're just the right age to keep me from falling into scrapes, is all."

"And you don't mind, about the hair?"

"What, did you think I wanted a beau whose hair was longer than mine like that rattlepate Warden? Or who spent an hour each day putting every curl in place like your friend Podell? But you, do you mind that I'm not . . ." Blushing, she held out the stocking.

"That's nothing a babe or two won't cure, but no, I don't mind. To me, you are perfect." And he closed the gap between them, and showed her how much he didn't mind. "I love you, Miss Audrina Rowe, just the way you are."

"And I do love you, Max, and have forever. But . . ."

He groaned. "Have pity, sweetheart. Just say that you'll make me the happiest of men."

She smiled, but said, "But you haven't asked my father."

"What? You never cease to amaze me. For such an independent little thing, I wouldn't have thought you'd be such a high stickler."

"I could never marry a man my father didn't approve, Max. And you've never even met him."

"I'm sorry, puss. I know you and your father are close. And you mustn't worry about him, you know, after we are married, for he'll be welcome to make his home with us or at any of my estates. Or we'll find him a curate to help here. Whatever you want."

"What I want is for you to meet Papa first. I always said I'd only marry a man just like him."

"Good grief, Dree, you're asking the impossible. By

all accounts your father is nearly a saint. I go to church and all, and try to support a great many charities. You don't expect me to give up the earldom and my fortune, do you?"

"Of course not, silly. Papa is everything good, but that's not what I meant about wedding a man like the one my mother did. She gave up her world for him."

"I swear I'll make you the same kind of loyal, devoted husband. And you won't have to give up anything."

"Just go meet Papa, then decide if you can be the man I always wanted."

Max whistled the whole way back to Dree's uncle's house from the vicarage. His heart was lighter than it had been in years, as he rode his great stallion through the wintery woods to claim his bride. Reverend Rowe had given his permission, finally, for Max to pay his addresses in form. Max had enumerated his titles and holdings, then the contents of his bank accounts. It wasn't until he revealed the contents of his heart, though, that the vicar had relented.

"Can't live without her, eh?" he'd asked, his eyes twinkling behind the lenses of his spectacles. "Aye, I felt the same way about her mother. Well, you've my blessing, if she'll have you."

"She'll have me, sir. She wants a man just like her father."

And they both laughed over a glass of sherry, the earl with less hair by the day, the vicar whose last hair had kissed his pillow good night some twenty years ago.

The Last Valentine

Friday

Mrs. Barrett was a late sleeper.

George the cat was an early riser.

As usual, George prevailed. Thus Martine, the Widow Barrett, groped for her black shawl in the cold February dawn and draped it over the shoulders of her flannel gown. Without candle, without slippers, and without coming fully awake, Martine stumbled down the stairs of her modest home on the outskirts of Chelmstead village and fumbled at the lock on her front door.

George complained at the delay.

"Oh, shush. I'm hurrying as fast as I can. And don't you dare awaken Mrs. Arbuthnot." Mrs. Arbuthnot was the elderly lady hired by Martine's father to act as her companion. Watchdog was more like it, though, Martine thought, or spy. The crotchety old dragon hated George. She wasn't particularly fond of Martine either. The only thing that made the woman at all bearable, besides knowing she had no choice in the matter, was the fact that Mrs. Arbuthnot never rose above the ground floor. Her ankles were too swollen and sore, from too many sweet rolls and sugarplums. She had taken over the morning room and a small parlor at the rear of the house, which was why Martine was trying to get her cold-numbed fingers around the latch at the front of the house. Martine did not wish to discuss having animals in the house, appearing downstairs in one's undress, or showing consideration and respect for one's elders—not at six o'clock in the morning. Not ever.

Not for the first time did Martine consider that her life wasn't precisely as she wished it either. The door open and George gone, she stared out at the barren winter landscape. Gray, everything was gray. The cloud-covered dawn, the shriveled bushes in her front yard, the stark, square houses of the village, her days and nights. No, this was not how Miss Martine Penbarton, privileged daughter of the Earl of Halpen, had planned to spend her life. Parties, travels, gowns, servants, and handsome gentlemen, those were the things she had dreamt on as a girl, not making her own clothes, doing her own baking and wash, growing her own vegetables, or helping Chelmstead's frail old vicar tend to his needy flock. She'd thought to have a houseful of infants. Instead, she got to teach a handful of farm children their letters when their families could spare them. She also taught Sunday school, mended altar cloths, and took tea with the matrons of Chelmstead village. Her only friend was George the cat, and sometimes she wondered about him.

Things could be worse. Oh, they could be a great deal worse, Martine reminded herself. Mrs. Arbuthnot never lost an opportunity to remind her either, of the sights they'd seen in London on their way to Chelmstead, four years earlier. Martine's father had directed the driver to take the hired coach through the worst of London's stews and slums, so she could see the women half-naked in the streets, begging or plying their miserable trade to filthy lechers and foulmouthed soldiers and falling-down drunks. Yes, things could be worse without the earl's grudging generosity. They could also be a great deal better, if he showed some mercy to his once-cherished daughter.

It seemed he'd cherished his own dreams of her marrying his heir more than he'd cherished Martine. When she refused, and disgraced herself in her rejection of Cousin Elger, the scandal was quickly covered up. Martine was bundled away to obscurity with Mrs. Arbuthnot to see she brought no further shame on the family. Meager provision was made for her welfare, but there were no luxuries, few comforts, and less forgiveness from her father. And now, four years later, Martine thought she could never forgive him for telling the world he had no daughter. What he had was no heart.

George was long gone about his own business of terrorizing the birds. Bess would let the cat back in when she came up from the village to cook and clean. She'd also start the fires, thank goodness, for Martine's bare toes were turning blue. She turned to shut the door and go back upstairs to bed. Her days were long enough without starting them at the crack of dawn.

As she turned, a scrap of white caught her eye. A folded note was wedged under the brass door knocker. Martine removed the paper and went inside. How odd, she thought, turning the note over as she made her way upstairs. It had no direction and no return address. The seal on the back was unidentifiable, to Martine at least.

Shrugging, she broke the seal and held the page closer to the window in her bedroom.

There is one week until Valentine's Day, she read. *I have waited this long to ask you to be mine. I will try to be patient until then.*

There was no salutation and no signature. Martine shrugged. The note was romantic, mysterious, and a mistake. The sender must have directed a messenger to the wrong house, for Martine had no beaux at all, much less one waiting any amount of time. Why would he wait, this unknown admirer? Mrs. Barrett was a poor but respectable widow, still wearing mourning for her soldier husband, who, of course, had never existed. That is, George Barrett had once lived, and died, but not in Martine's vicinity. Her father had simply borrowed the fallen cavalryman's name for his fallen daughter. She'd named her cat after him; it was the least she could do.

At any rate, no other man had approached her in her tenure at Chelmstead. Perhaps that was Mrs. Arbuthnot's sneering influence, for she would be out of a position should Martine find a husband. Or perhaps it was Martine's aloofness that discouraged the local merchants and tenant farmers. She was attractive enough, and only two and twenty, but she truly wasn't interested. Her life might be easier with a prosperous husband, but she doubted she could ever love again, and she could have married Cousin Elger if she wanted a loveless marriage.

No, the note had to be a mistake, or someone's idea of a joke. But the paper was too rich and thick for any local apothecary or haberdasher, and the writing was too well formed for the farmers and sheepherders. Martine doubted that even the neighboring squires had such fine, educated hands.

Perhaps the note was meant for Mrs. Arbuthnot, she thought, and had to stifle a giggle at the idea. 'Twould take a brave man indeed to get his courage to the sticking point to approach that formidable misanthrope. No wonder he needed another week.

Was it truly just a week until Valentine's Day? Martine supposed so, although she'd need to look at a calendar, since all her days seemed to melt together. And Valentine's Day, well, that was for starry-eyed lovers and young dreamers, not for ones such as she. No, never again.

She tossed the note onto her desk, climbed into bed, and pulled the covers over her head. She didn't even think of her own, long-lost love. Not once, not after four years.

Saturday

It has been four years, the new note said. *I can wait another six days to ask you to be mine, but oh, how impatient I grow, knowing you are so near. I think of knocking on your door, sweeping you up into my eager arms and riding off with you, but no, this time I shall do the thing properly. Sweethearts' Day it shall be, dearest, the day the birds select their life mates. And yet I find I must ask, am I waiting in vain? Are you spoken for? If there is someone else in your life, if you would rather I left, please, sweeting, put me out of my misery now. I swear your happiness means all to me. Here is a rose as a token of my affection. If you accept it, I can keep on waiting, keep on hoping.*

She should take that rose and snap its stem, shred its petals, scatter them to the ground, then stamp on them. Instead Martine clasped the note and the flower under her shawl and fled back inside and up the dawn-lit stairs, like a thief in the night. She told herself that such a perfect red rose was too precious to destroy. Not even Squire's succession houses boasted such prize blooms.

Of course, Martine knew she couldn't place it in a vase in the drawing room, not without facing an interrogation that would put the Spanish Inquisition to shame.

77

Even in Martine's own bedroom, Bess was liable to notice and wonder where the widow came by such a flower in the dead of winter. It would be a shame, but Martine would just have to press the rose in her Bible, where no one could see it. For now, though, she climbed into her bed, the flower still clutched in her hand. Thank goodness the thorns had been removed.

This morning Mrs. Barrett was not going right back to sleep.

Four years, the note had said. Four years. It had to be him, then, not some prankster or bashful beau or mistake in the note's delivery. In fact, he must have been watching the house, to know Martine was the one to put the cat out at dawn each day. There'd been no names again either, so he must be aware of Mrs. Arbuthnot, too. This way, if the letter blew away or got into the wrong hands, there was nothing to point in Martine's direction. Lud, if the old besom caught a whiff of the rose's perfume, Martine would be locked in her room, if she didn't get tossed out in the streets. And Digby would be hung up to dry on the clothesline. Oh God, Digby.

Four years. They had been four long years for Martine. She'd stopped crying over him ages ago, telling herself he was not worth her tears, until she was convinced. It didn't take long. The dastard had left her in the middle of their elopement. He'd taken the money her father had offered and then decamped, leaving her disgraced and devastated. Lord Halpen still wished her to marry his heir. Cousin Elger still had damp hands and rotten teeth. She refused. Her father refused to have her in his home, declaring that his honor forbade him to offer any other gentleman such soiled goods in marriage. While she was still numb with heartbreak and disillusionment, the earl packed her off, in hastily fashioned widow's weeds, to this little backwater village, where she could rot for eternity in genteel poverty or marry some schoolmaster. He cared not which, so long as she lived a virtuous life. The threat of being cut off entirely was there, with no resources, no recommendations for employment, no capabilities beyond a smattering of education. She had been reared for marriage, by heaven. How could she make her own way in the world?

Her home, her family, her future, all gone with Digby Hines. Now here he was, sending her valentines! Martine wiped a treacherous tear from her eye and stroked the velvety petals of the rose. She should take it outside right now, before Mrs. Arbuthnot arose, before she had to watch it wither and die like her love had done at Digby's betrayal.

Of course, she didn't love Digby anymore. Why, she couldn't recollect what he looked like, except for his fair hair and blue eyes. And what did an eighteen-year-old know of love anyway? she wondered now at twenty-two. Perhaps it was just infatuation, perhaps the thrill of a forbidden romance, perhaps merely an escape from her father's rigid demands.

She hardly remembered Digby, but she did remember love. There in her solitary bed without even the cat to keep her warm, Martine recalled how it felt to be in love, believing one was loved in return. As sweet as the scent of the rose, it was, and as short-lived. But she did not take the flower back outside.

Sunday

My precious, how relieved I am not to find my flower left out in the cold, with my dreams. And now there are only five more days to be got through, although it still seems an eternity. Each day brings a new agony to me. I swore not to rush my fences, not to ask for your hand until Valentine's Day, the perfect day for lovers, but now I live in fear that you'll turn me down out of hand, that you've never forgiven me for leaving you. I find I've turned craven overnight, but I'd rather face another four years of French cannons than see the look you gave me that last day.

How can I explain? I loved you. You must believe me, for I have never stopped loving you. But I had nothing to offer, my dearest, only the most uncertain of futures. I couldn't live on the outskirts of society like so many other men without fortunes, gambling to pay the rent, outrunning the bailiffs every few months. And I could not ask you to live that way. Nor could I face being supported by my wife's income, whatever it was. Blame my pride for leaving you, not the depth of my affection.

I was determined to make a success of myself in the army, to prove my worth, but how could I ask you to follow the drum, such a tender bud that you were? And *how could I marry you, knowing I was leaving, perhaps never to return? I could not, in good faith, so much as ask you to wait for me, not such a young and beautiful woman, so full of life. A soldier's fate is too uncertain. At least I do not have that on my conscience.*

I leave you this box of ribbons, paltry stuff, I know, except they might help to prove that I am not a coward, not entirely, anyway. Can you accept this token, and my poor excuses for whatever unhappiness I may have caused you?

Digby a soldier? Martine thought her memory must be faulty indeed. He'd been everything he said, when she met him in London at her come-out, a regular Bond Street beau. His shirt collars were up to his ears, and his debts were up to his eyeballs, but so were all the other young men's. Digby was the most handsome, the most elegant, with the most practiced charm, she realized later. And she was the wealthiest heiress Out that Season.

Yes, she'd thought Digby a coward for not standing up to her father when the earl rejected his suit, and again, when Lord Halpen found them at that inn halfway to Gretna. Digby had cowered before her father's wrath, and fled with his gold.

But here was a carved wooden box full of medals, ribbons and such, a hero's horde. Martine lit a candle in her room, to spread them out on her bedstead as she reread that letter again and again. What did they represent? An act of valor, a battle won, an injury, a promotion? There were so many, he must have been in constant danger, trying to prove himself worthy of her. Oh, how she had misjudged him!

He must have taken her father's money, she realized now, and bought himself a commission. She knew nothing of his ambition before that, Martine reasoned, because he would have been too proud to confess his dream, knowing he couldn't afford it.

The woman she was now would have followed him

to the ends of the earth, but he was right: the pampered debutante she was then could not have cooked hares over campfires or washed his uniforms. She would not have exchanged her gay London life for the squalor of a barracks, not by half. He was right, but not in leaving her, not in going away without an explanation, not in leaving her heart so bruised she could never love again.

Could she forgive him? Loyalty to king and country demanded it. Digby must have become one of England's bravest soldiers, risking his life countless times. The least Martine could do was hear him out. She put the ribbons under her mattress, to think about what she should do.

Martine had never been ready for church so early before. Her hair was neatly combed under her lace cap, and her black wool gown was freshly pressed, twice. She spent the opening hymn searching for him through the pews of the little church, her eyes seeking any fair-haired man, in case she hadn't recognized him on the first glance. There were no soldiers in uniform, no well-muscled, weathered gentlemen, no strangers whatsoever. Mrs. Arbuthnot pinched her arm and hissed at Martine to stop acting like a long-necked goose. Martine had to be content with adding his name to her prayers, thanking God for his safe return.

That night when she called George in after his last foray, Martine left a token of her own outside the door. She should return the ribbons, she told herself, and not get involved. No, she should return the ribbons and add a ha'penny, to show what she thought of him for leaving her for her father's money. He'd been bought off, for goodness' sake! Instead she carefully placed one of her old hair ribbons from when she wore colors next to the front step. The pretty blue ribbon with pink roses embroidered on it would seem to have been dropped by accident, or windblown there, in case he didn't come.

Then she had to pry it out of George's claws. "It's not a toy, confound you." She shrugged and tied the bow to the door knocker. She'd be up with George long before Mrs. Arbuthnot saw this evidence of her depravity.

Monday

What noble forgiveness, my precious. Thank you from the bottom of my aching, anxious heart. I could only think of buying you these bonbons, in return for your sweet generosity of spirit.

Martine opened the parcel she'd found on the stoop that morning, along with the letter. The box contained chocolate bonbons, sugared walnuts, pink marzipan hearts with iced flowers on top. Such delicacies hadn't come Martine's way in ages. She popped one in her mouth. Chocolates before breakfast; now, wasn't that decadent! Mrs. Arbuthnot would have apoplexy. Martine had another candy, then returned to the letter.

But I prayed you could forgive me, being so warm and loving. You are what we were fighting for in Spain, you know, cara mia. And you are what I dreamt of day and night, in those wretched tents and blood-soaked fields. I think the image of you was all that kept me sane amid the horrors of war. I wrote to you almost every day, you know. No, how could you, for I never mailed the letters. I couldn't, when I didn't know if I was ever to return, or if I'd come back less of a man, maimed beyond recognition like so many of my fellows. But I did write, whenever there was a pause in the

*shooting, when we were back at headquarters, when I
was recuperating in the hospital tent from my, thank-
fully, minor wounds. I told you a hundred times that I
should not have left, that I should have stood by you no
matter what, that war was a fool's gamble. I was such
a green youth. I didn't know what I held until it was
lost. Youth lasts but moments on a battlefield, and now
I have come back, all of me in working order, to claim
what should have been mine.*

*There are only four more days to suffer through until
Valentine's Day. I can do it, hold to my resolve, sweeting, because you deserve the most romantic valentine I
can conjure.*

Martine dabbed at her eyes with the corner of her
bedsheet and ate another bonbon. That dear man. How
proud she was of him, her hero, and how guilty she felt
for having to struggle to remember the tone of his voice
or the smell of his cologne. She hadn't thought of him
in months, and then only for the what-might-have-been,
not the who it might have been with. She hadn't read
the war news for his name on casualty lists or recommendations. She hadn't prayed for his safe delivery. Instead she'd cursed his very existence, as the self-serving
villain who ruined her and deserted her.

"Oh, my love, can you ever forgive me?" Martine
sobbed. But obviously he had; he was sending her letters and flowers and promises. And candy. She sat up
and wiped her eyes. What was she going to do with the
candy? Pigs would fly before she shared them with
Mrs. Arbuthnot, even if Martine could explain them
away as a Valentine treat she'd purchased. If she left
them here, Bess would find them, or George. There was
nothing for it but to eat the candies, every last one of
them.

"You ain't coming down with something, are you,
gel?" Mrs. Arbuthnot demanded over lunch.

"No, ma'am. I'm just not very hungry today."

"Well, eat anyway. I can't abide finicky chits, you know, so don't you go putting on airs."

"No, ma'am. In fact, my mind has been distracted. I have been thinking of putting off my blacks. It has been four years, and I am sick of these dreary, depressing rags."

"Twenty-two years I've been in mourning for Mr. Arbuthnot. It shows respect. For you, it shows your respectability."

Martine put down her napkin. "Our neighbors know me for a decent, proper widow. There is no need to keep up this charade."

"No!" Mrs. Arbuthnot hissed, making sure Bess had returned to the kitchen. "You'll keep on pretending to be a devoted, grieving widow all your days, gel. Keep you from tossing your bonnet over the windmill again." She went back to her mutton.

Martine could feel her cheeks grow warm, but she insisted: "Mrs. Arbuthnot, if I wished to toss my bonnet, it would not matter what color it was, black or red with purple ostrich feathers. I have saved some of my housekeeping money, and I am going to purchase material for a new gown this afternoon."

"I shall write to the earl immediately after lunch!"

"And say what, that I am sinking into a life of sin because I wish a new gown?" Martine sat up straighter. "Go ahead. But be sure to ask yourself where your next meal is coming from, after he cuts me off without a farthing." She stared pointedly at the mounds of food on Mrs. Arbuthnot's plate, then rose from the table. "Forgive me, I find I am not feeling quite the thing after all."

She was feeling just fine when she walked to the village shops that afternoon. Even Miss Fletcher at the Emporium noticed the roses in her cheeks, the sunshine in her smile, the bounce in her step. "It's a man, I wager," she whispered to her sister while Martine inspected the bolts of cloth.

"And about time, too, I swear."

The sisters were so pleased for the gracious young widow who'd added so much to their little community that they wrapped a few bits and scraps of ribbon and lace along with the rose velvet dress length Martine chose, in case she wanted to make a valentine for her sweetheart. Martine thought she just might.

Meantime she purchased a bunch of dried rosemary with her hoarded pennies. For a new recipe she wanted to try, she told the Fletcher sisters and Mrs. Arbuthnot, who intercepted Martine in the hall before she could make her way upstairs with her parcels.

"Can't taste any rosemary in this chicken," the old woman complained at dinner.

"Perhaps I didn't use enough." And perhaps she didn't use any, preferring to braid the rosemary into a small heart-shaped wreath she'd hidden in the bushes. Rosemary was for remembrance; everyone knew that.

After the meal Martine cut and pinned her new gown while Mrs. Arbuthnot muttered dire warnings about the wages of sin. At nine o'clock, Martine went to the kitchen to make their tea. Mrs. Arbuthnot had hers with a tot of rum every night, to help her sleep, she said. She never seemed to have any problems with that, declaring it bedtime as soon as the tea things were put away. So Martine put on her cape and put out the cat. She stayed outside, the door partly open so she could find her wreath, then find a place where Digby would notice it, but not think it was a decoration for the door. Then she stayed out, wondering if he was near, trying to feel his presence.

"What maggot have you got in your brainbox now, missy?" Mrs. Arbuthnot shouted from the parlor. "Leaving the door open and standing outside in the middle of winter!"

"Someone in the village today said a storm was coming. I'm just trying to see if it feels like snow."

It didn't. It felt like springtime in her heart.

Tuesday

*M*artine was up before George. Considering that she'd stayed up half the night basting the gown—and looking out her bedroom window—that was quite a feat. She hadn't got much sewing done, and she hadn't seen or heard a thing, so she couldn't sleep for hours even when she blew out the candles, wondering if he was coming back at all.

He had come, though. The wreath was gone, and in its place were two packages tied in silver paper, atop a sealed letter. She opened the letter first.

I remember, my precious darling. I never forgot. Three more days, and we can share the memories and make new ones.

I want to buy you the sun and the stars, but I cannot, so I had to be content with these trifles for now. The combs are from Spain, for I thought of you so often there, and how your silky hair would look in the señoritas' style. And the book is because you deserve sonnets written to your beauty, but I am just a soldier, not a poet.

I must tell you that I do not intend to stay a soldier, if you will have me. I do not intend for you to follow the drum any more today than I did four years ago, and now there is no reason. I have proved myself in my own eyes, if not the eyes of the world, and I have prospered. I might not afford to buy you the moon, but I can purchase a small estate for us somewhere, with a few acres to farm. No more paltry cottages. My saved-up pay, a tidy competence I receive, and an unforeseen inheritance make me a man of substance, if not wealth. Yes, I am puffing off my prospects, sweeting, in hopes that you will look more favorably on my suit.

Other officers spoke of their futures, of travels and Town life. I have had enough excitement to last the century. I want nothing more than to settle down, to put roots into the land, to see things grow finally, instead of the death and destruction of war. I want to watch our children run and play where the air is clean and good, with you by my side. I would take you to London if you yearn for the glamour—I would take you anywhere, dearest—but oh, how I have dreamt of the peace and quiet and contentment of a country home, a family. In three days I'll ask you to share that with me.

A home, a family, a loving husband—and two presents! What more could a woman want? Martine swore she would not weep, not again. But she hadn't received a single present since she'd been in Chelmstead, except for the occasional dead mouse from George. Now here was Digby Hines, the man from her past, offering her a golden future, showering her with gifts.

The combs were intricately carved ivory masterpieces that demanded she unbraid her long auburn hair and try them in different styles. The book was Shakespeare's love sonnets, in hand-tooled leather with gilded pages.

Martine's resources hadn't extended to books, so this was even more precious. She'd even had to let her subscription to the lending library expire, because Mrs. Arbuthnot declared novels to be the devil's own handiwork. Oh, the old dragon would love this! "Shall I compare thee to a summer's day" indeed!

Of course, Mrs. Arbuthnot must never see the book.

Martine could leave it here in her bedroom, among her old volumes on the shelf, for Bess couldn't read and wasn't interested in learning. But the combs had to be hidden. Even if Martine swore they were hers from before, Mrs. Arbuthnot would instantly recognize them as something foreign and heathen, therefore improper. With sore regrets, Martine buried the beautiful ornaments under the velvet lining of her jewelry box. She went back to sewing on her dress, a smile on her lips.

She had to have Bess's help pinning the hem that afternoon.

"Oh, you do look a treat, Mrs. Barrett," her housekeeper cooed. "Will you be going to Friday's assembly up in Wolford then? They're having a special do for Valentine's Day, don't you know. You're sure to take some handsome gentleman's fancy, I swear."

"No, we won't," Mrs. Arbuthnot answered for Martine with a thump of her cane. "It's not fitting. Anyone with a few pence can attend the assemblies. A lady could find herself dancing with turnip pickers and plowmen. That's whose eye she'd catch in that indecent gown anyway. No, we shall not attend." She glared at Martine, daring her to challenge the decision.

Martine loved to dance, but no, the festivities in Wolford were not part of her Valentine's Day plans. She was more concerned with the style of her gown. Indecent? The dress was velvet, not some filmy, near transparent gauze, and it had long sleeves and a high neckline. There were no flounces or scallops at the hem, no embellishment at all beyond a darker pink ribbon at the high waist.

Even Bess was taken aback. "Why, I seen Squire's wife wear a lot less fabric, with a lot more to put in it, iffen you catch my drift. Even her daughters as is just out of the schoolroom wear their thin muslins cut down to there, with less to show off than Mrs. Barrett. Nothing improper as I can see."

Mrs. Arbuthnot snorted. "It's pink! Pink is for debutantes—or harlots."

That night Martine put a folded paper outside the front door and hoped the snow would hold off another day, or that Digby would come soon to fetch it. Her efforts at watercolors were never quite successful, but today, in her haste—well, a dampening could not improve the picture. She'd wanted to leave him something, to give something back to the one who was giving her so much, in tokens and in joy. Even if her finances permitted, though, and Chelmstead's shops provided, she wouldn't know what to purchase for him, to show she shared his hopes and dreams. So she'd painted a landscape of a white house on a hill, with six, no, ten chimneys, surrounded by fields and cows. At least she'd meant them as cows, but they ended up looking more like trees, so she'd put apples in them. Yes, an orchard would be lovely. The sky was blue, with no clouds; the grass was new-green, except for one corner where the colors ran together, so she made a pond. And flowers everywhere, dabs of bright colors, at any rate. She'd put a tiny couple in the doorway, watching even tinier children who were chasing a dog, a ball, and a water drop. They all wore pink.

Wednesday

*H*e'd left her a music box. The music was unfamiliar, but two porcelain doves turned on the base when she wound the key. *You make my heart sing,* the note read. *Oh, how I wanted to hold you close to me when I saw the painting, but I have wanted to hold you, touch you, kiss you, ever since we parted. I can wait the two more days, my dear heart.*

Was that your light I saw late into the night? I watched from outside, wondering if you were lying abed, reading the poems, thinking of your humble, hopeful suitor. We should have been together in your white house, reading aloud by the fireside, sharing a cushioned sofa. But I fear my imaginings wandered, and I confess we would not stay long on that sofa, reading. Too well do I remember your exquisite body. How I ache to hold your rosy softness against me. There was no softness in Spain, querida, *only you in my dreams.*

Let there be no untruths between us: there were other women. I am just a man. But none were you, none moved me to my soul, with none did I feel the love in lovemaking. Two more days, my darling. Two more nights.

Martine's cheeks were flushed, even under the bedcovers. Goodness, she thought, Mr. Shakespeare was not half so stirring as Digby Hines. Her rosy softness? Oh my. Yes, her bones were turning to mush at the very thought of . . . of what he was thinking. She must be a fallen woman indeed, to become overheated by a letter.

Martine was a bit surprised at Digby's ardor. They'd only made love twice before her father found them. The first time was messy, awkward, painful, and uncomfortable. The second time was simply uncomfortable. Just when she was beginning to feel there might be something appealing about this act, it was over. And messy. From the giggles and snatches of conversation at the ladies' sewing circles, she gathered not every woman felt that way. She was willing to try to enjoy herself. From her reaction to Digby's warmish letter, Martine doubted she'd have to try very hard. At the very least, she vowed, if he got so much delight from the act, she could gain her own pleasure from giving him his.

That night she left out a valentine. Two pink velvet hearts, scraps from her new gown, trimmed with lace bits and ribbon roses, were firmly joined by enough glue to hold together a piano.

Thursday

*W*hen Martine broke the seal on the letter, a gold heart on a chain fell out.

Please wear this, until I can lay my own heart at your feet tomorrow.

When shall I come? Must it be a proper morning call lasting a proper twenty minutes, or shall I come for tea with you and your duenna? I am wishing you can be rid of her, so I can take you in my arms, but I want no blot on your reputation, my dearest. Should I meet you at the assembly in Wolford then, and greet you among strangers? Tomorrow would be the longest day of the year in that case. Tell me your wishes, cara, *I'll make them mine.*

Tomorrow was going to be the longest day in history if Martine had her way, but only because it was going to start the earliest. She was not about to meet him for the first time in four years in full view of the population of Chelmstead or Wolford, or under the gimlet stare of Mrs. Arbuthnot. That harridan would never leave them alone long enough to pledge their love, much less seal the pledge. Martine fully intended to give Digby the only valentine she had left to offer, herself in her new pink gown.

Martine put an extra measure of medicinal rum in Mrs. Arbuthnot's tea that night. Then she let George in, but didn't lock the door, and didn't snuff the candle in the upstairs hall. Outside was an old, broken clock, as if left for the trash. The hands were set to a minute past twelve. She wrote "midnight" above the twelve, to make sure he understood. Then she went upstairs to change.

The pink gown whispered around her hips, the gold heart nestled between her breasts, the combs pulled her auburn curls back off her forehead before letting them tumble down her back. Would he still think she was beautiful? Her figure was fuller now and her face thinner, paler, except for the spot on her chin from eating all that candy. She blew out another candle.

The fire burned low in her sitting room, a bottle of wine and two goblets waited nearby. George was snoring. Martine was pacing. The ormolu clock on the mantel must have stopped running, so she shook it to make the hands move faster.

Then she heard what she'd been waiting for, the sound of the door handle turning. She waited at the head of the stairs, in the shadows, merely whispering "Shh" when he appeared. She could just make out the scarlet uniform as she beckoned him up the steps and into her sitting room. Then she turned and threw herself into his waiting arms. His lips came down on hers as his hands pressed her against his firm length. Her hands wove through his hair, pulling him even closer, and the earth shook.

"Oh, Digby," she sighed against his chest some minutes later, just as he murmured, "Rosalyn, my Rosalyn," into her hair.

Martine's eyes snapped open. "Rosalyn?"

His arms dropped to his sides. "Who the hell is Digby?"

"D-digby Hines," she sputtered uncertainly, "the man

who has been sending me valentines and presents." She fingered the chain around her neck.

"I've been sending the blasted valentines!" he shot back in a harsh whisper. "But who the deuce are you? They told me in the village that the Widow Farrell still owns this place."

"She does; I lease it from her."

The look on his face was so comical, Martine had to laugh. It was either that or cry. She crossed to the mantel and brought him the glass of wine. "Here, sir, I think you are in need of this."

He took a swallow, then ran his hand through his hair, making even more of a mess than Martine had. It was dark hair, and curly, nothing like Digby's, she realized as she studied him while he drank the rest of his wine. He was taller, too, broader-shouldered and more muscular, with a bronzed complexion from his years on the Peninsula. Digby had always appeared pale, colorless from his hours in drawing rooms and gaming parlors.

The officer put down the glass and gave her a tentative smile. "I'm afraid it will take a deal more than a glass of wine to fix this argle-bargle. I've really made a deuced mull of it, haven't I?"

Martine shook her head. "Not by yourself, sir."

"You are too kind, Miss . . . ?"

"Barrett. Mrs. Barrett."

"And Mr. Barrett? No one in the village mentioned him. Is he going to come bursting through the door at any minute demanding I name my seconds? It needs only that."

"No, Lieutenant Barrett won't be coming, Captain." She figured out his insignia.

"My apologies, ma'am, for being so clumsy. I should have known, for everyone spoke of the pretty widow lady at the edge of town. I just assumed they meant . . ."

"Rosalyn."

He nodded. "Do you know where Mrs. Farrell is now?"

The poor man was already so devastated, Martine hated to give him more bad news, but she had to tell him that Mrs. Farrell had married a wealthy merchant from Wolford. "All of Chelmstead was still talking about the wedding when I moved in, four years ago in April."

"April! I just left in February!" He moved toward the window to stare out at the night. "She hardly waited for my ship to sail."

"I'm so sorry." And Martine was, seeing his shoulders droop. "You must have loved her very much."

He gave a hollow laugh. "I loved a dream. I was miserable, lonely, and afraid, so I found a memory to cherish, that was all. Do you know, I should have realized something was wrong when I overheard those men in the pub singing your praises. They said the young widow at Farrell's place was kind to everyone despite her own hardships, full of goodness to those less blessed. A real lady, they called her—you. I was thrilled, you may be sure, thinking that Rosalyn had changed for the better, for that was precisely what I wanted in a wife. Rosalyn was a selfish, greedy minx. She made no secret of the fact that she married her first husband for his money."

"Then you are well out of it."

He turned back to Martine, where she had taken a seat next to the fireplace. When she nodded toward the matching chair the captain sat and asked, "But what about you, ma'am, waiting so patiently for your Digby? This must have been a crushing blow. By God, I am sorry. What, was he missing in action, that you thought he'd been returned to you?"

"Digby, missing in action?" Martine was confused.

"Lieutenant Barrett, your husband."

"Oh, that wasn't Digby, that was George. I never knew him." Hearing his name, the cat jumped into Martine's lap. "Good George," she crooned. George purred, the officer stared.

He got up and brought the other wineglass over to Martine, along with the bottle. "I think you need this. The shock and all."

She shook her head, blinking away a tear. "No, it does make sense. And like you, I should have known better than to think Digby was suddenly so caring and thoughtful. Digby Hines was the man who ruined me. We were eloping, but my father caught up with us half-way to Gretna. Digby let him, I think. I was an heiress, you see. Papa told Digby he'd never see a brass farthing of his blunt, if we married. So Digby let my father buy him off. I haven't seen him since."

"The bastard ought to be drawn and quartered."

Martine shrugged. "George Barrett was a dead soldier my father chose from the casualty lists to give me some respectability—and a name that wasn't his—when he established me here."

Before taking his seat again the officer looked around at the skimpy furnishings, the meager fire. "In grand style, too. You haven't been very fortunate in your men-folk, have you, Mrs. . . . Miss . . . ?"

"Miss Penbarton, I was. Martine." She chuckled. "Anything but Rosalyn."

He smiled back, flashing even, white teeth. "You're a regular trump, Miss Martine Penbarton Barrett. Any other female would be swooning or weeping or throwing things at me."

"Oh no, I'm made of sterner stuff."

Now that his shock was wearing off, the officer was taking note of precisely what she was made of. Martine could feel his eyes travel from her head to her toes, with a long stop at the gold heart between her breasts. They were very nice eyes, a soft brown, with laugh lines at the corners. Still, Martine blushed and made to remove the necklace.

"No, no. You must keep it for your trouble. Besides,

I could never give it to anyone else. But that's a minor point. Miss, ah, Martine, we have to decide what we're going to do."

"Do? There is nothing to do. I'll go fetch your ribbons—you really should be wearing them with pride—and you'll go off to find your cozy nest in the country. Hopeful mamas will be trotting their daughters past your gates before the cat can lick his ear."

He frowned at the prospect. "But what about you? I've seen how you live." He waved his hand at the room, the house.

"Oh, I'll get by. Perhaps I'll start getting out more."

"And perhaps you'll be ruined."

She had to laugh. "I am already ruined."

"Not here in Chelmstead, you're not. Everyone admires you. But what if someone saw me come in? I was careful, but you never know. What if some late-night reveler sees me leaving? Or if your dragon wakes before I'm gone? What would your fond parent do then?"

Martine gasped and clutched the gold heart in her hand. "He'd cast me off without a shilling. Oh dear, please leave now. Take your gifts lest someone find them. Here—" She pulled the combs out of her hair, letting the silky curls fall to her shoulders.

He drew a deep breath at the sight of the reddish tresses in the fire's glow. "No, there is another way. We could get married."

"Married?" she squawked, then clamped her hand over her mouth. "I . . . I don't even know your name!"

"Damn and blast," he muttered. "Cursed barracks manners. My apologies." He stood and snapped to attention. "Captain Aden Kirkendale of His Majesty's Cavalry, ma'am, at your service." He bowed, then dropped to his knees next to her chair and reached for one of her hands. "Martine, hear me out. I realize we don't know each other very well." At her raised eyebrows he corrected himself: "All right, we know each other hardly at all, but arranged marriages are made all the time between strangers, strangers with less in common than we have. We've both been disappointed, and we've both been alone too long. I know you share my dreams. Your painting—"

"Was a mess, a childish effort."

Aden patted his jacket pocket. "A masterpiece which I wear next to my heart. Don't you see? I fell in love all over again, but with the woman the villagers talked about, the one who was honest and loyal and kind, everything a woman should be, everything the mother of my children should be."

"No, no, you are just being honorable, in case my reputation is destroyed." Martine tried to reclaim her hand, but he held fast and stroked it, still kneeling at her side, sending shivers up her arm.

"Silly puss, have you looked in the mirror? Any man would be thrilled to have you across the breakfast table for the rest of his life. I would count myself the most fortunate of men if you accepted my offer, and I'd spend eternity trying to make you happy. I'd understand, of course, if you don't feel that you could come to care for me."

Now Martine patted his hand and laughed softly. "I have to admit that I fell halfway in love with your letters. You were so noble and so gentle, someone to trust and lean on."

"So lean on me, Martine. The rest will come, I swear." He brought her hand to his mouth and kissed her fingers, then the palm. "You felt that kiss when we first met, I know you did. It was perfect."

"The earth shook."

"No, I'd stepped on the cat. But there was a spark. We can build on that, too. Trust me, Martine. We'll make each other happy. And if not, if we find we don't suit after all, I'll just go back to the army. There's always a war going on somewhere. You'd be provided for no matter what."

This was insane! And very, very tempting. "But . . . how?"

Aden grinned. He could tell she was weakening. He touched his pocket again. "I have a special license right here. We can call on your vicar first thing in the morning and be on our way by noon unless you have a lot to pack."

Martine shook her head no. "I don't have much, and most of my clothes are for mourning, not a honeymoon."

"Good, then we'll stop off in London and buy us both new wardrobes, since I have only my uniforms. We could take in the theater and the opera while we consult some land agents about property and I arrange with the War Office to resign my commission. Would you like that?"

"I love the opera."

"Me, too," he lied with his fingers crossed behind his back. "See how well we're matched? Are you convinced?"

"You're sure this is what you want?"

For answer Captain Kirkendale reached inside his uniform and brought out a small box. He opened it to reveal a gold ring with a square-cut diamond in the center, surrounded by a cluster of rubies in a heart shape. He put it on her finger. "Will you make me the happiest of men, dear Martine, and be my valentine, now and forever?"

"Now and forever," she repeated, then met his lips in a kiss that seared their souls together. "Just don't step on the cat."

Love and Tenderness

Chapter One

$\mathcal{A}$ girl expected some degree of anxiety on her wedding night. Senta Tarlowe, abruptly and henceforth Senta Morville, Viscountess Maitland, had anticipated the butterflies in her stomach spawned by awkwardness and inexperience. After all, she hardly knew this stranger who now held her future and the hem of her first lacy nightgown in his large hands. Senta was even prepared for the pain her scarlet-faced mama had stammered about, before disappearing into the carriage on her way home this afternoon. What the new Lady Maitland hadn't expected, not in her most vivid imagination or most horrific bad dream, was the sight, over her husband's shoulder, of a specter at the foot of the bed.

Senta knew the figure wasn't real flesh and blood because she could see the flickering flames of the fireplace behind him, right through his cloth-of-gold suit, wide belt, and high boots. Whereas she'd convinced herself to suffer silently through the indignities and uncertainties of the marriage bed, ghosts, ghouls, or heavenly visitations did not count.

Since her husband, Henley, Viscount Maitland, had been pleasantly absorbed in nibbling at his young bride's tender earlobe, nuzzling at her silky neck, nudging her neckline lower, his ear was in close proximity to Senta's open mouth. Just as he was murmuring, "Oh, Senta, how I want you. I need you. I—" she shrieked.

The sound could have shattered the crystal chandelier at the Royal Opera, much less the eardrums of one slightly befuddled bridegroom. Henley, Lee to his friends, clamped his hands over his ears. "What the deuce—"

The apparition also clamped his hands over his ears. "What the hell—"

He was no angel, then, which was less than reassuring to Senta. "Wh-what do you want?" she managed to gasp out.

The glimmering figure merely shook his head in a confused manner, but Viscount Maitland was either less rattled or more aggrieved. "What do I want? That should be obvious even to a blasted vir— gently bred female. I want to make love to my wife!"

Senta had taken the moment of Maitland's distraction to pull the covers back up to her chin, both for modesty's sake and the sudden chill in the room. Now she stared from the viscount's scowl to the phantasm's befuddlement, back to Maitland's expectant "Senta?"

Maitland didn't see the ghost. He was right beside her, and he didn't see a flickery gold-suited gentleman with rings on his fingers and a huge diamond in his belt buckle. Somehow that made Senta's panic worse, that she was alone in this nightmare. She pulled the covers over her head and cried, "Go away!"

Lee pried the sheets out of his wife's trembling fingers and drew them away from her face. "You'll suffocate, goose. Now listen, Senta, I know you aren't used to any of this, and it's natural to be frightened."

Frightened? She was staring at him in abject terror, her eyes so round she looked like his aunt's pug. "Come on, Senta, you seemed to be enjoying yourself." Lee knew he was. "We'll go nice and slow." Any slower and he'd embarrass himself for the first time since he was sixteen. The viscount gritted his teeth, reminding himself for the thousandth time that night that she was young and innocent. "And tomorrow we'll laugh about the whole thing."

He might laugh, Senta was thinking, but by tomorrow she could be an empty corpse, her soul sucked out of her by this demon who was staring around the room. Too scared to speak now, she could only shake her head, no. Oh, great heaven, no.

"Then you really want me to leave? I'll go if you want me to, Senta, for I would never force any woman, especially not my wife. But you are my wife, and you'll have to face this sooner or later. You know I want an heir."

Her husband might be a near stranger, but he was big and strong and alive. Oh Lord, don't let him leave! All she could croak, though, was, "Not you. Him."

"Him?" The viscount jerked himself upright, pulling Senta's covers every which way. While she scrabbled to shield herself from the fiend's now-interested view and the cold draft, Lord Maitland tore at his hair. "I knew there had to be another man! I just knew it! Why would such a beautiful young woman still be unmarried after two Seasons in Town? And why would she give herself to a man twelve years her senior? I should have known it was too good to be true." The viscount got out of the high bed and reached for his robe on the floor. "What, was he unacceptable to your family, or was I simply the bigger prize with the title and Maitland fortune? Lud, don't tell me they forced you into the marriage. No, I don't think I could face that tonight. Hysterics are bad enough."

Lee crammed his arms into the robe without looking back at his gasping bride, whose own arms were held out beseeching him not to leave. He wrestled the sash at his waist into a knot. "You're in no state to discuss this tonight, and I'm afraid I'm not either. We'll have to straighten it all out in the morning. Until then, my lady, my sincerest regrets." And he slammed out of the room, barefoot, stomping right through the dark-haired, broad-shouldered wraith.

Senta passed out.

When Senta awoke, the room was in darkness, the fire having burned down to a few embers. What a terrible dream she'd had! As she lay there, though, shaking her head to clear it, Senta recalled that it hadn't all been just a bad dream. She'd actually made a shambles of her wedding night, sending her bridegroom fleeing in high dudgeon and disgust, all on account of her foolish wedding jitters. Bridal nerves, that was it, and too many toasts at the small wedding breakfast, with too little food in her stomach.

She'd made a proper mull of it, Senta reflected, wiping a tear from the corner of her eye. Now Lord Maitland—she really had to start thinking of him as Lee—must think she was a ninnyhammer or, worse, an unwilling bride. Of course he was insulted, although how he could think her dear parents would force her to marry a man of their choice was beyond her. Mama and Papa loved her. They would have given her another Season if she hadn't settled on the viscount this year, and even another, if it meant a happy marriage for their only child. They had never even pressured Senta to accept the viscount, despite Lord Maitland's standing as one of the premier prizes in the Marriage Mart. They didn't have to. Senta had fallen top over trees for the quiet gentleman, as soon as she got over her awe that Lord Maitland had singled her out for his attentions.

The viscount was rich and titled, yes, and handsome enough that when they danced she was the envy of every female in the room. The other gentlemen—those not already wearing corsets—tried to hold in their stomachs, such a fine figure did he present. But none of that would have mattered to Senta. Lord Maitland was a favorite of the ladies without being a dissolute rakehell, a favorite of the gentlemen without being a profligate wastrel. He was a Nonpareil in her eyes. And he was kind.

He was much too kind to let suffer through the rest of the night thinking that his silly bride didn't like his touch. She'd liked it very well indeed. Tomorrow's talk would be embarrassing for both of them, having to discuss bedroom matters in the harsh glare of day. 'Twould be far better to get the explanations over with tonight, while darkness could hide her blushes. And while she still had the courage.

Senta reached for the candle by her bedside and struck the flint. She tossed back the covers, put one foot out into the cold air—and there he was. Not Lord Maitland, but the see-through shade.

She was *not* going to scream, Senta told herself, stuffing her hand in her mouth to make positive. She'd disturbed the servants once this night, she was sure. Heaven only knew what they were already thinking, or how she was to face them in the morning. By comparison, facing this . . . this spirit had to be easier. Senta took her hand out of her mouth, put her chilled foot back under the covers, and studied her visitor as it—no, definitely he—slept in the nearby chair. The seat's upholstery stripes wavered through his outline.

His long legs were casually stretched in front of him, tightly encased in the gold unmentionables. Heavy dark hair had fallen onto his forehead, giving him a much younger look. He had high cheekbones, a perfect nose, thick eyelashes, and a mouth a Greek sculptor would have cried for. He was, in fact, quite, quite beautiful, like a fallen angel. Asleep, he seemed too innocent to be any minion of Hell, though. Besides, Senta was still alive and unharmed. Therefore he had to be a mere ghost, which was not to say a gently bred female liked to find that her new home was haunted, but a peripatetic predecessor was preferable to a demon. Senta couldn't begin to imagine from which century this Maitland ancestor hailed. And she'd made a careful study of the portrait gallery this past month. Most of the gentlemen were sandy-haired, like her husband. None of them remotely resembled her somnolent specter. Furthermore, Senta firmly believed that the Morville clan, dead or alive, was too mannerly to cut up a lady's peace.

"Sir?" she called softly, determined to direct this lost soul on his way.

He came awake with a start, blinked, and brushed the hair out of his eyes. He noticed Senta sitting up in her bed, the candlelight reflected off her ivory skin through the lacy gown she wore. One side of his mouth curled up in a smile. Definitely no angel, Senta thought, pulling the bedcovers up.

"Sorry 'bout that, ma'am." He shook his head. "Sorry 'bout the whole thing."

So he did have some manners. Maybe he was a Maitland ancestor after all. Senta couldn't place the accent. The long sideburns were somewhat in the military mode, though, and there had been a lot of Morville officers. "Who . . . ?" she began. "What . . . ?"

Now he scratched his head. "Don't rightly know, ma'am. I just kind of show up places. Sometimes I remember bits and pieces of stuff. Other times something sounds familiar, but I can't quite put my finger on it."

"Surely you know your own name."

He curled his lip again. This time it looked more like a sneer than a smile. "You'd come as far as I have, you'd be all shook up, too."

He cocked his head, as if hearing distant music instead of Senta's correction: "All shaken up."

He said, "I've been racking my brains all night."

"Could you be a Lord Maitland?"

"Maitland? No, that doesn't sound right. It's more like a turnip. Parsnip?"

"Your name is a vegetable?" Senta pinched herself under the covers. Unfortunately, it hurt. She was awake.

110

"Uh, maybe it would help if we discovered *what* you are. You know, ghost? Guardian angel?" She had to add, "Devil?"

"You mean a ghoul? Like me?"

"I," she corrected automatically. "A ghoul such as I."

He stood up, looking confused. "No, ma'am, I'm no bogeyman. I'm a legend. That's it, a legend that never dies."

"A legend? Like King Arthur?" Now Senta dredged her mind. Parsnip? Parsley? Sage? "I know! You must be Father Time. You know, t-h-y-m-e."

"No, that don't sound right either."

She thought some more. "Saint George? How about Parcival? That sounds somewhat alike. Could you be Sir Parcival who went after the Holy Grail?" She'd always thought the story was fiction, but she supposed such a hero could take on a life of his own, more or less.

His brows were furrowed. "It sounds close. You know, like a name on the tip of your tongue. I think what happened is my memory got left somewhere else, and just hasn't caught up yet. Hell, sometimes I feel as though if I could just remember a few more details, I could go on home."

Senta made a silent toast to that. But her visitor was obviously distressed, so she asked, "Why don't we just call you Sir Parcival for now?"

"I don't know about that Holy Grail stuff, and the 'sir' don't sound right either."

"Then you aren't a knight?" she asked in disappointment.

"Not even a Pip."

Senta bit her lip. With all those jewels, he was certainly of the upper classes. "Then are you an earl? A duke?"

He raised his perfect chin. "Ma'am, I'm the King."

Senta was fairly certain no King of England ever looked like this. "King of what country?"

"More like rock, ma'am."

"You're the King of Gibraltar?" Senta didn't think there was such a thing. Then again, history had never been her favorite study. "Did you actually sit on a throne?"

He put his head in his hands. "Don't ask."

She took a deep breath. Here it was, her wedding night, and she was entertaining a ghost, and a crazy one, to boot. Well, the mad King of England thought he was the palace cook or some such, so Senta supposed her ghost—legend—could be as balmy as he wanted. If he just left. "Ah, besides seeking your lost memory, was there some particular reason you arrived here?"

He looked around. "Reason?"

"You know, like vengeance, or to right an old wrong." Senta thought back over ghost stories she used to hear at school. "If you weren't buried properly, or didn't receive last rites. A mission."

"I don't rightly recall, ma'am. I suppose I'm here to make things right for you."

"Nothing was *wrong* for me until you got here!"

"Didn't look that way to me."

"You were watching?" Senta gasped. Thank goodness he couldn't see her flaming cheeks.

He shrugged. "Nothing much else to do. You were a-lying there like a sacrificial virgin. And what about this forced marriage and some other guy? You got someone else's bun in the oven, sister?"

"That's Senta. And what do you mean, someone else's— Oh." She figured it out. "Of course not. And my marriage was no such thing. It wasn't even an arranged match, like that of many of my friends."

"Arranged?"

"You know, where the parents decide to join two estates or two fortunes. The brides have to hope their fathers make the right choices for them."

"The fathers get to choose? Hmm."

"Yes, but mine wasn't that way at all. Lord Maitland

even asked me if it was all right to ask my papa for permission to pay his addresses. He thought I might be pushed into accepting him, once he made his formal offer. But I wanted to marry Viscount Maitland, very much."

"He don't seem to know that."

Senta chewed on her thumbnail, which she hadn't done in ages. "No, he thinks it was a marriage of convenience, I suppose." Sir Parcival, for want of a better name, was looking more confused than ever. Senta didn't know why she was telling her troubles to a transparent Bedlamite, but she continued anyway: "A marriage of convenience is when a titled gentleman, for instance, marries a girl with no family connections, but a large dowry. He gets the money; she gets the title."

Sir Parcival's lip curled. "We don't call that convenience; we call it commerce. They don't have to love each other at all?"

"They don't even have to like each other. There are many matches in the ton like that, where both partners go their separate ways. I'd never have a marriage like that."

"But your bridegroom would?"

Senta chewed on her fingernail some more. "He started attending debutante balls and Almack's for the first time in memory, and everyone said it was because he needed an heir after his younger brother's death. He is two and thirty, you see. It was time to start his nursery."

"So he wanted a broodmare. What was he offering as stud fee?"

Senta ignored the vulgarity. It was all too true that any unattached female would have tossed her bonnet over the viscount's windmill. She sighed. "He has everything. Wealth, title, lands, influence, looks, intelligence, honor. He could have had any woman he wished."

"But he chose you."

She smiled, and hugged that thought to herself. Lord Maitland had chosen her, with merely passable looks, undistinguished family, and average portion. And she was delighted. She'd wanted to dance and shout and sing, but there he was, so serious in Papa's library, telling her that he would not announce any understanding yet, in case she changed her mind. In fact, he didn't want her to decide until after the end of the fall Little Season. If she was still willing, she and her family could spend the Christmas holidays at his country property, to see if she might be happy there. He was no absentee landlord, he carefully warned her, and the place was somewhat of a moldery old pile sorely in need of a woman's touch. He'd asked again on Christmas eve, and again she'd said yes, and he'd given her the family betrothal ring, finally.

"He must have thought I'd make him the most biddable wife." Senta fumbled for a handkerchief so she could blow her nose. "And I meant to be, I swear. Now look at the mess I've made!" she wailed.

Sir Parcival was scowling. "You stop that blubbering, sister. I hate when women cry. Did you ever tell the man you loved him?"

She sniffed. "My name is Senta. And . . . and I don't love him. I hardly know him. My parents approved, and he was everything kind."

His lip curled again. "Sure, you don't love him and I'm Prince Charming."

Senta didn't think so, not with that sneer. "How could I tell him such a thing? He's so proper, he made sure we were never alone. But he should have known! When he asked if I wanted to wait till his year of mourning was up in the spring to have the wedding, so I could have a big affair at St. George's, I said no. I told him I'd rather get married right now, right here at his home, before Mama and Papa left after New Year's, rather than wait. That should have told him I wasn't just interested in all his grand connections. He should have known!"

Sir Parcival was up and pacing. "I reckon that's my mission then, to tell him you love him."

"You can't do that! I'd die if he thought I loved him when he . . . he only wants a mother for his sons."

"So what I have to do is get him to love you back, right, and make this a real marriage?" He moved toward the door.

Senta gave a watery laugh. "You? You don't even know your own name, and he can't see you. Oh, it's all such a mess." She started weeping again for her lost dreams.

"Doubts, huh? I've had a few." Sir Parcival stepped through the closed door. Before he disappeared, he called back, "Little sis— Senta, don't you do . . . Don't you do that . . . Don't you cry."

Chapter Two

"*D*amn and blast," the viscount muttered. "I knew it would never work!" Lord Maitland was in his library, in his undress, in despair. He poured himself another cognac from the cut-glass decanter on the cherrywood desk and tossed it down. "How could I ever expect a jewel like Senta to fall for a dry old stick like me?"

She was a diamond, his new bride, beautiful to look at, beautiful on the inside, too. When he first came up to Town in the fall, determined to find himself a wife and fulfil the responsibilities of the succession, Miss Senta Tarlowe caught Lee's eye immediately. She was such a gay, spirited young thing, always smiling, pleased with whatever entertainment the day offered, from lavish balls to simple country picnics. She didn't blush, simper, or bat her eyelashes, nor did she put on the airs and affectations so many of her peers wore in pretend sophistication.

Lee had watched her at various functions before even seeking an introduction. He noted how, as often as she was the center of a knot of admiring beaux, just so often she was like to be found in a gaggle of female companions, belles as well as wallflowers. Other times she seemed content to sit quietly with her parents.

Her reputation was spotless. He'd made inquiries, as far as he could without seeming obvious. No one had the slightest ill to speak of Miss Tarlowe, except a few disappointed suitors who found her too particular in her notions. Maitland couldn't fault her for that: getting legshackled was a serious enterprise. He'd allowed himself a year for the business.

It wouldn't be the grandest match of the Season. The Tarlowes were solid country gentry, while the Maitlands were used to running the country. Nor would the gal bring any great riches or vast estates, which suited Lee to a cow's thumb. He had more than he could do handling his own properties and investments. Any dowry Miss Tarlowe brought would only be settled on her children. His children.

For the first time since his brother Michael's death, the idea of becoming a tenant for life grew more appealing. As he watched her swirl through the paces of a *contra danse* with some spotted youth, Lee was convinced Miss Tarlowe would make him an excellent wife.

He approached cautiously at first, a dance here, a not-so-chanced meeting in the park there. Lee knew what a storm of gossip his least interest would produce, and wished to spare Miss Tarlowe that discomfort. But there were so many other, younger, men trailing at her skirts, men with no greater needs than to sit at her feet and write poems to her golden locks. Lee sat on two Parliamentary councils and wrote briefs for the Foreign Office. Nor could he dally on in London, worshiping her eyebrows like those sprigs, not when the Corn Laws were wreaking havoc in the countryside.

But what if she accepted one of them? Suddenly all those other fishes in the matrimonial seas were blowfish or barracudas or big-mouthed bass. It had to be Miss Tarlowe.

And she seemed to favor his suit. The viscount wasn't naive enough to be surprised, yet he was delighted and relieved nevertheless. He moved slowly, quietly, not about to frighten her off with protestations of devotion and endless passion. And he gave her every opportunity to retreat without dishonor. He was even willing to wait six months to give her another Season to look around, to decide if he was the best she could do. It might have killed him, but he gave her the chance.

She hadn't taken it. She'd taken him instead.

Lee poured out another glassful and this time sipped it slowly. No, he thought now, she'd taken his title and fortune and social standing, not the man. Not the man she'd just thrown out of her bed.

That man's feet were getting cold, so he tugged on the bellpull. He knew the household was up, for he could hear scurrying and whispers beyond the library door. Hell, he'd be glad if Senta's shrieks hadn't awakened the sleeping Morvilles in the family crypt.

When he heard a scratch on the door, Lee's heart leaped up, but it was only a footman with an armload of firewood. Then his valet came in, handing over a pair of slippers without meeting his master's eyes. Even the butler, Wheatley, who was as much a fixture at the Meadows as the suits of armor in the hall, entered silently. He made room on the desk for a pot of coffee and a cup, not too subtly moving the cognac decanter aside.

Lud, what the staff must think of him now! Lee shook his head. Years of being a fair and generous employer, earning their respect, were wiped out in one night. What kind of beast brutalizes his sweet young wife into hysterics on their wedding night? Lee couldn't imagine. But he was sure his servants could. By tomorrow the tale would be all over the countryside, too. Trying to stop the gossip would be like holding the ocean from the shore. He shoved the coffee aside and reached for the cognac. "Hell and damnation, is it possible to make more of a mess of this night's work?" he asked himself.

Lee didn't see the gold-clad figure glide through the wall, nor did he hear Sir Parcival's answer: "Un-uh, reckon it's impossible." The spirit had drifted through the vast mansion looking for the viscount, catching giggling maids and leering footmen. "Man, this place is bigger than ... bigger than ..." He shook his head. "By the grace of God, I wish I could remember."

Lord Maitland, meanwhile, decided on the coffee after all, to warm him. He shoved the cognac back and filled a cup of the strong, hot brew. He'd had too much to drink already today, perhaps enough that he could blame some of the night's fiasco on the devil in the bottle. He wasn't one to overindulge in the usual course, so perhaps all the toasts at the wedding breakfast had him a trifle disguised. If his head had been clearer, maybe he wouldn't have frightened poor Senta so much.

Sir Parcival gazed longingly at the decanter, but shrugged and strolled about, admiring the rows upon rows of leather-bound volumes. He was even more impressed with the tiger-skin rug in front of the fireplace. Lee didn't notice.

Thunderation, the viscount cursed to himself, he'd known Senta was frightened. Hell, he'd been quaking in his boots himself, or out of them, as it were, nervous about making the first time pleasant for her. He wasn't inexperienced, not by a long shot, but the women he was used to were usually even more experienced. Most assuredly Viscount Maitland was not in the practice of deflowering virgins. He'd even had a cold bath before knocking on the door of her bedchamber, to dampen some of his ardor. It hadn't worked a bit.

He couldn't wait to make her his, to tie her to him with bonds of passion, to express his love in a way his fumbling words never could, to make her forget every other man who ever existed. Maybe she'd even get to like him, just a little. But no, he'd rushed his fences. His head hadn't been clear enough to exert control over his wayward body. Lee blamed himself for the whole debacle, for having too much on his mind to pay attention to Senta's anxieties. Then he told himself it wouldn't have mattered at all, if she had another man on her mind.

Lee sighed and pulled open the top drawer of his desk. Reaching toward the back, he pulled a hidden lever and another, secret drawer opened. The viscount withdrew two folded notes. "I didn't make her happy," he lamented aloud. "Didn't make her like me. Now I can't even protect her from scandal."

Sir Parcival stood behind Maitland's chair to see what was bothering this jackass so much he didn't get back upstairs and make love to his wife. "Hell," Sir Parcival muttered, "you wouldn't find me down here catching my death, if I got a woman waiting upstairs." He cocked his head. "Nah."

Lee was studying the two notes. Fine, he thought, his wife had two lovers; he had two blackmailers.

Sir Parcival leaned over his lordship's shoulder to peer at the notes. He read one and whistled through his teeth, causing the viscount to tug at the collar of his satin dressing gown to avoid the draft. He couldn't, for Sir Parcival whistled again, after he read the second message. "Those ain't no love letters," he drawled. "No wonder your hand's shaking like a leaf on a tree."

The first letter, written in bold but elegant script on fine-quality paper, advised: *If you do not wish your bride and the public to hear the true facts concerning the death of Lieutenant Michael Morville, send five hundred pounds to the Seven Swans posting inn, in London, attention, Mr. Browne.*

The missive had arrived at the Meadows right after Christmas, via the troubled hands of Lee's London secretary, John Calley. Lee hadn't paid the demand, of course. Once you paid an extortionist, he became your pensioner for life. Besides, you could pay and pay, and still have no guarantee that your family skeletons would stay in the closet. Lee wouldn't put his trust in finding any honor among such thieves as would steal a dead man's integrity.

Instead he'd sent back with his trusted secretary a thick letter to Mr. Browne, three pages folded and sealed with the distinctive Maitland crest. Let the dastard think his blood money was inside.

The pages were blank, while Calley had enough blunt to bribe everyone at the inn from the porter to the potboy. Someone ought to be able to identify Mr. Browne when he retrieved the letter, quickly enough for the men Calley was hiring to follow him. If Lee had to spend more than the five hundred pounds in rewards and bribes, it would be money well spent, to defang the viper. Let Calley just find the snake's name and direction, then let Mr. Browne see how he liked the payment Lee was planning to give him.

So far, there had been no report back from London. Nor any gossip.

The other note was on common stock, and had arrived today before the wedding. No, 'twas past midnight. Lee's wedding day had come and gone. It was already yesterday now. He could only shake his head at the waste, and look back at the second message. This one was written in ill-formed letters, which could have disguised a gentleman's handwriting, even a woman's, but Lee didn't think so, from the caliber of the threat: *I know what really happened to your little brother. I'm at the inn. We need to talk.*

This villain was a fool, thinking to get away with extortion in Maitland's own home village of Mariwaite, where every stranger was immediately suspect. The townspeople had been loyal to the Maitland family for centuries. If the fellow dared breathe a word against Michael, he'd be lynched before Lee could get to him, which would be a deuced shame.

Not that the viscount meant to pay off this gallowsbait, any more than he would the muckworm in London. And he didn't need to talk to anyone about his brother, for he already knew more details than he wished. Details that he thought—prayed—he could carry alone to his own grave. It was not to be.

Maitland stood and carried his coffee to the mantel, over which hung a picture of the late viscountess, his mother. She was wearing a rose-colored gown in the style of twenty years ago, and she was smiling down at the child at her feet. Another boy, himself, stood rigidly at her side, already serious and solemn at ten. The baby frolicked with a ball at his mother's skirts. Lee remembered the nursemaids endlessly chasing after toddling Michael to return him to the sitting, while the artist scowled. Lee had stayed put, hating every minute of it, because the heir to Maitland knew his duties. Mama just smiled.

Oh yes, Lee knew how Michael had died in Portugal. Thank goodness their mother had passed on before she had to know.

The official version, because of Maitland's money and influence, and because the army couldn't afford another scandal right now, was that Lieutenant Morville was accidentally killed when his rifle discharged while he was cleaning it. It was just one of those quirks of war, they said, that a young man could serve with distinction through all those bloody battles and retreats, even survive the fevers and fatigues of the occupying army, then succumb to a misfired bullet. Frightful loss and all that. There were even rumblings among the condolence-callers of shoddy weapons, misspent appropriations. Lee had nodded, accepting the sympathy, because the heir to Maitland still knew his duties.

The story was a lie. The generals knew it; Lee knew it. They thought they were the only ones, that they could get away with the fabrication, so Lee could bring the body back and bury Michael next to their parents in the family plot with some degree of honor. It wasn't a hero's burial, but neither was it a traitor's hanging, or a suicide's ostracism.

For in truth Michael, that little cherub playing so sweetly at their mother's feet, had done them all the courtesy of blowing his own brains out before the army got a chance to court-martial him. He'd led his own men into an ambush after selling information about their movements to the French.

Lee still couldn't believe it. He had a hard enough time believing dashing, daring Michael was never coming back, much less that he was a turncoat. But the evidence was there, laid out by Michael's commanding officer: the French script found in his bunk, the gambling chits he'd signed, the casualty reports of a supposedly secret mission. Most damning of all was the general's own report of the bullet to the temple. Innocent men don't kill themselves.

Why hadn't he sent home for money if he found himself up River Tick? Lee had asked himself a hundred times. He'd never refused Michael anything, not even the commission the young hellion begged him to purchase. All the young officers gambled; that was no great failing. No, Michael knew his sins were so great that suicide was the only solution.

But it hadn't been a solution at all, not one the army or Lord Maitland could live with, so they'd devised a death by misadventure. Lee could hold his head up, with his family name still untarnished, while he searched for a woman to give him heirs to replace his fallen brother. That was his duty now.

He went courting and found a pure, innocent girl, he thought, with the light of heaven in her blue eyes. Well, they'd both cheated on their wedding vows.

Senta's soul wasn't quite so unsullied, although he still believed her body was. So far. On the other hand, he'd offered his fine old name, which was in reality as tarnished as a pinchbeck teapot. If she'd married him for the exalted social position, she was in for a disappointment as bad as this wedding night was to him.

The truth was bound to get out now, even if he paid.

If two men knew the truth, there would be others. It would be a scandal of epic proportions, and a blot on Lee's own honor, that he lied and laid out donations to the war effort to get Michael a decent burial.

No matter, Lee had no intention of paying. But he did intend to do what he could to repay the blackmailers for his anguish.

"I'm not going to let this night be a total waste," he vowed out loud as he left the library, calling for his clothes, his pistol, and his carriage, in that order.

Wheatley protested from his position of aged family retainer. "But, milord, there's flurries starting. Who knows, but we could have a blizzard by morning. You can't go out in this, and on your wed—"

"I'm going," Lee snapped back before Wheatley could finish that thought. "I'm only going as far as the inn in the village, old man." Let the whole staff think he was going to drown his sorrows in local ale or in the arms of a willing tavern wench. Lee didn't care. He was going to get some satisfaction out of this evening.

Sir Parcival, his brow furrowed, long fingers tapping out a silent tune on the desktop, stood staring at the two notes. He didn't know what he was doing here, or how to get back to something familiar. He figured that since Senta could see him and no one else could, he must be here to help her. He hunched his shoulders. How? He didn't even know what her husband intended to do out there in the night.

He stared at the letters as if the answer lay in their words. If he could just figure out the meanings and motives behind these two notes, he'd know better how to help. Then maybe he'd get his memory back and go home.

He tapped the London missive. "Number one's for the money. And number two"—he looked down at his fancy high-heeled, pointy-toed boots—"is for the snow."

Chapter Three

"*B*ut, my lord, it's the middle of the night. Your wedding night." The landlord of the village inn was practically in tears as he tried to seat Viscount Maitland in his one private parlor.

"I bloody well know what night it is. Everyone seems bent on reminding me!" Lee was having none of the landlord's hospitality as he stood in the hallway brushing the snow from his greatcoat's shoulders and stomping his frozen feet. "What room?"

"But ... but you can't go wake up the paying customers!" The landlord dropped a plaintive "My lord" at the end.

"Can't I? Just watch! Either you tell me which room holds the man who sent a note up to the Meadows yesterday, or I'll go kicking down every door upstairs until I find him. And I wager whoever's paying Bessie to warm his bed tonight won't be half pleased."

Nor would that other couple who stopped here on account of the snow. Cousins, they said. The kissing kind, the innkeeper swore.

"What room?" the viscount demanded again, snapping his coiled driving whip against his thigh. His lordship wasn't known for his temper, but the innkeeper wasn't known for his foolhardiness either. "The second door on the right."

Lee took the stairs two at a time, calling back over his shoulder, "See that my horses don't take a chill. I won't be long."

Sir Parcival was still outside in the snow, staring up at the wood sign swaying above the doorway of the inn. As usual, there were no words, from the days when almost no one could read, just the carved and painted outlines of a hart and a drake. "The Deer and the Duck?" He curled his lip. "Man, these folks have no imagination."

It didn't take much imagination to figure what Lord Maitland had in mind when he pounded on the second door to the right with the handle of his horsewhip.

"It's Maitland."

A scratchy voice answered: "I need a minute, m'lord, to put on my—"

A minute was too long for Lee. He pushed the door in, rushed toward the bed, and grabbed for the figure sitting there wiping his eyes.

Lee lifted the man in one hand by the collar of his flannel nightshirt. "If you say one word," he warned, brandishing the whip in his other hand, "I'll kill you. Do you understand?"

What was not to understand? The man nodded as vigorously as he could dangling from the viscount's fist. That was when Lee realized his captive had almost no weight to him. "What the deuce?"

He dragged the fellow toward the open door and the hall lamp. What he saw did not make him happy. The mawworm was missing most of his hair, a few of his teeth, one of his legs, and part of his ear. Besides that, he was half Lee's weight and twice his age. "Damn and blast, I can't kill an old cripple."

"I never thought I'd thank them Frogs for what they done to me," the old man croaked.

Lee shook him once and dragged him back to the

126

bed. "Shut up, I said." He lit a candle, then slammed the door on the innkeeper's anxious face. Sir Parcival came in anyway, but no one noticed, except for the sudden chill. There were some noises in the hall as the landlord reassured his other guests that the inn wasn't on fire or under attack. A dog was barking out in the stable, but soon even that sound died, until all that was left was the viscount's whip tapping against his breeches, the old man's raspy breathing, and Sir Parcival humming "Cherry Ripe," which he'd heard a maid singing.

"Thunderation!" Lord Maitland swore, shivering with the cold. "What else can go wrong in one night?"

"With you? Anything, if you keep going off half-cocked," Sir Parcival commented with that half-arrogant look as he leaned against the window ledge, staring out at the falling snow.

Lee wasn't looking, or listening. He was searching the room's meager contents for weapons. The chest of drawers contained a comb and a razor, a change of linen, and two handkerchiefs. The peg behind the door held a suit of rough but serviceable clothing. Lee patted the pants pockets to make sure they were empty, then tossed the worn breeches to the oldster, who had taken the opportunity to strap on his wooden leg.

"It's like this, m'lord," he began.

Lord Maitland was checking under the mattress. He tossed a thin purse he'd found there onto the bed and took a threatening step closer to the graybeard. "I told you to keep your mouth shut!"

"Then how you going to find out about—"

Lee's whip snapped inches away from his nose. "I can take a fly off my leader's ear at a full gallop. Do you have anything else you'd like to lose?"

The man buttoned his lip, and his woolen pants.

"Now, listen," the viscount ground out after opening a frayed carpetbag to feel among the folded shirts and pants. "I don't want to hear any of your filth except the answers to the questions I'm going to ask. Is that clear?"

The old man spit between the gap in his teeth, perilously close to the viscount's feet. "Clear as the mud on your boots, m'lord."

"Don't push your luck, granfer. It's your years keeping you alive, not my patience. That's in short supply tonight. Now, what's your name?"

"Waters, m'lord, Private Jacob Waters, late of His Majesty's Army."

"Too late, it looks like."

"Aye, but they wasn't handing out pensions, and I never had nothing to come home to. So I stayed on." He knocked on the wooden leg. "Till they tossed me out when I wasn't fit to be cannon fodder no more. Shipped me home with a pocketful of silver and a coach ticket."

It was a common enough story, and not one to make decent Englishmen proud, how the country treated its returning veterans. Nor was it an excuse to turn to a life of crime.

Waters went on, now that the viscount seemed to be listening: "It weren't so bad when we wasn't seeing action. I got to make extra money taking care of some of the younger officers' weapons and uniforms and such. Them as didn't have a batman of their own. That was how I got to know Lieutenant Morville. Kept his billet for him, I did. Your brother was—"

Waters found himself dangling above the ground once more.

"Don't you even mention my brother's name again, do you hear me?"

"I bet they can hear you clear 'cross town," Sir Parcival put in, for no one's benefit but his own. "If you'd just listen to the old warhorse, we could all go home and get into warm beds."

Oblivious, Maitland had lowered the soldier back to the ground. "Who else knows?"

"That I took care of Lieu— the young officers? Everyone in the company, I'd guess. Weren't no secret."

"Damn you, who else knows how he died?"

Sir Parcival nodded. "Now, that's more like it, man."

Private Waters must have thought so, too, for he let out a deep breath. "Well, there's this señorita, Mona."

"The devil take it, I don't want to hear about your lightskirt."

"You got it wrong. She was your bro—" The look on Maitland's face made the private's voice trail off. "Mona's no lightskirt."

"Stubble it. I want to know who you told in London."

"London? I called at your place there, but they said as how you were in the country. I didn't talk to nobbut the butler."

"My own butler's not blackmailing me, by Jupiter!"

"Blackmail, is it?" The man rubbed his stubbly chin. "That why you're so prickly? You think I—"

"I think that if you don't have an accomplice, you have a competitor. I'll see both of you rot in hell before I give either of you one shilling. Now, who else knew the truth about my brother's death? Someone who might be in London now?"

"I guess it must be one of those toffs Mona saw. They come out to headquarters to fetch home a relative as got wounded. An officer. She didn't get their names, and I was on maneuvers. But they was the ones what rigged that card game what made the lieutenant—"

"Not anther word!"

"But we come all this way to tell you the story. We figure one of those nobs was the—"

"I've heard enough." Lee waved his fist under the smaller man's chin. "You'll never tell your story to anyone, do you understand? I've managed to give my brother more honor than he deserves, and I mean him to keep it. Why, if I had my way, I'd put you on a ship to

129

New South Wales along with the other scum of the earth."

"Here now, gov'nor, you can't do that!"

"Of course I can. I'm the magistrate."

"But I didn't do nothing!" Private Waters wailed.

Lee was sick of the whole thing by now. "You threatened a peer of the realm. That's enough to get you transported." He started throwing the man's things into the carpetbag. "Be happy I'm only sending you to my plantation in Honduras. You can tell your story there till you are blue in the face."

Sir Parcival was shaking his head. "Blue Honduras? Nah."

Waters, meanwhile, was hobbling around, trying to keep his belongings away from this madman. "Honduras? Threat? I only wanted to make sure you knew the truth about your brother."

The viscount tossed the old man his coat. "I know all there is to know about my brother," he said through gritted teeth.

"You don't neither of you know nothing about t'other. He thought you was a fair, intelligent man, and you believe he could be a trai—!"

Lee stuffed the fellow's nightcap in his mouth, bundled him into a blanket, and tossed him over one shoulder. He picked up his whip and the satchel with his other hand, and stormed out of the room, down the stairs.

The landlord was standing there, mouth agape. Lee tossed him the carpetbag while he reached into his pocket for some coins. He put a golden boy into the man's hand. "This should settle Private Waters's bill and any other questions you might be thinking of asking."

"Nary a one, my lord, nary a one. Good evening and . . . and my felicitations on your wedding."

Lee just grunted as he threw Waters and his valise onto the seat of his curricle when the stableboy brought it around. He gave the boy the nod and tossed him another coin. Then he cracked his whip, this time well over his horses' heads, sending them off at a trot through the snow-covered lanes.

Sir Parcival was perched behind, where the tiger would ride. He was staring back through the swirling snow at the inn sign while it was still visible in the light of the lanterns kept burning to either side of the door. "The Stag and the Scoter? The Buck and Wing? Yeah, that must be it. The Buck and Wing. Not bad."

The village had a tiny gaol, a shed behind the livery where prisoners could await trial. The viscount didn't take Waters there, not to spew his filth into any passing ear. Instead he drove through the village, then down the hill to the shallow valley where some of his tenants had their cottages. Beyond that he turned the curricle onto a side path that took a shortcut through the home woods. The snow was falling softly, but the geldings were surefooted and the moonlight was sufficient. The only sounds were the jingle of harness and the horses' breathing.

In fact, Lee couldn't help thinking that this could be a lovely drive if it were his wife tucked cozily at his side to share the carriage blanket. Instead he had a footless ex-foot soldier next to him. And a chill down his spine as if the Devil rode at his back.

He drove through one of the clearings that gave the Meadows its name and reined in the horses at an empty gamekeeper's cottage. The windowless back room had a padlock, to keep out mischief-makers and poachers. Here was where the viscount deposited his prisoner and his bag.

"There's a pallet and some blankets. I'll start the fire in the other room so you'll get some warmth, and someone will be out in the morning to bring food. Take off the leg. You aren't going anywhere." Lee looked around at the neat little cottage while Waters, protesting the order, protesting his kidnapping, and protesting his innocence, removed his peg leg.

"You had only to ask." His lordship put the wood and leather contraption on top of the mantel, in the outer room. "If you were in need, I would have found you a cottage like this, just because you took care of Michael."

"I didn't come begging for no charity. I got some blunt put by. I only wanted to see justice done."

"At what cost? And how many lives ruined?" Lee shut the back door on the old man's ragings. "Go to sleep, Private Waters. If I find your friends in London and put them out of the extortion business, too, who knows? Maybe I'll reconsider and just send you to Ireland."

"But what about Mona?" Waters shouted as he heard the lock click shut.

"Mona? Oh, your Spanish whore. If she wants to go to Ireland, she can go, too."

"Mona ain't no whore. She's a lady, and your brother was going to . . ."

Maitland drove off. When he got home, Wheatley was waiting in the hall to remove his master's greatcoat, as if it were two in the afternoon, not two in the morning.

"Dash it, I can let myself into my own house and see myself to bed, Wheatley," the viscount complained as he handed over his gloves and hat, feeling guilty about keeping the man from his rest. "I've told you a hundred times."

"Yes, milord. But that's what you hired me to do."

Maitland nodded. "Well, as long as you're up, I'll need you to locate our most trustworthy footman. He'll be bringing food and supplies out to a prisoner at the old gamekeeper's cottage in the morning. I don't want him talking to the man, and I particularly don't want him talking about the man."

"Our people do not gossip, my lord."

"I did not mean to disparage your staff, Wheatley. Whoever you select will need to keep watch over the cottage until I can get to London and take care of a bit of business."

"Is he a, ah, desperate criminal, my lord? Should the footman be armed?"

"He's older than dirt, and only has one leg, dash it, or I'd have beaten him to a pulp. He'll be gone from here as soon as I can arrange passage out of the country for the dirty dish. Notify the stable I'll want the closed carriage first thing in the morning."

"In the morning." Wheatley stared somewhere over Lord Maitland's shoulder. "And Lady Maitland?"

Lady Maitland. He'd forgotten he was a married man. What an insult his leaving would be to a new bride! And how embarrassing she'd find the household's pretending nothing was wrong. But there was nothing for it. He had to go to London. The War Office was bound to know what young officer was fetched home the week Michael . . . died. If not, they could dashed well find out. Besides, he couldn't trust himself with Senta. While he was here, while she was his wife, he was going to keep wanting her.

"Lady Maitland must be asleep by now. I'll leave her a letter. She'll understand."

Sir Parcival fell off the pedestal where he'd been making the acquaintance of a long-dead Sir Morville slumbering in his suit of armor. Understand? When cow's milk turned blue!

Chapter Four

*H*e was leaving her. The letter had been brought up with Senta's chocolate and toast. She'd asked for breakfast in her room rather than confront Lord Maitland over his kippers and eggs this morning. After the mortification of last night, she needed more than a fresh dress to face him.

Her husband had gone out last night. Senta's bedroom overlooked the carriage drive. He'd returned sometime before daybreak, while she huddled miserably awake in her cold bed. Lord Maitland had been so disappointed in her, he'd had to leave the house in the middle of a snowstorm.

Senta had spent the entire night thinking of how she was ever going to make things right. How could she explain to such a serious-minded, rational man like her husband that she'd been frightened by a ghost? Or whatever that figment of her imagination and indigestion called himself. Maitland was sure to hurry home for that—to see her locked away in Bedlam! Fairy tales come to life, by George! Next thing she knew, Beowulf would be chasing Grendel through the corridors of her dreams.

Well, now she wouldn't have to think of another excuse for her skitter-witted behavior. He was gone.

His letter spoke of urgent business in London. While he was supposedly on honeymoon? And oh yes, he'd added a brief personal message: While he was in London, Lord Maitland intended to speak to his solicitor about obtaining an annulment. Personal indeed! He did not believe, the viscount wrote, that nonconsummation on its own was grounds enough to negate a marriage; it was bound to be a consideration, though, when he sought the annulment because their vows were already forsworn. If the fact that she loved another man didn't sway the courts and the clerics, he wrote, a few generous donations would. It seemed to Senta, as her teardrops made blurry tracks down Maitland's letter, that whereas money couldn't buy love or happiness, it could surely purchase his freedom.

Lord Maitland hadn't put it quite that way, of course. No, what he wrote was that he wanted what was best for her, with no discredit to her name. Whatever gossip arose would be a nine days' wonder, especially since most of society's gable-grinders were away from London in the dead of winter. Her speedy remarriage to a man she chose for herself would put paid to any scandalbroth. She wasn't to think of what effect an annulment might have on his, Maitland's, reputation. Her happiness was all that mattered.

How kind, how honorable, how thickheaded could one man be? If Lee Maitland were here right now, Senta swore she'd throw something at him! Herself. She would force him to see that *he* was the man she wanted, and none other.

Unless he was just looking for an excuse to get out of a misalliance. Miss Nobody from Nowhere was no match for the noble scion of the Morville dynasty. Why, she knew nothing about running a grand household or holding a man's interest. She couldn't even keep her own husband for one night.

And now what was she supposed to do? Wait around for him to toss her back, like a fish too small to keep? She didn't feel she had the right to begin her reign as mistress of the Meadows, not when it was to be one of the shorter tenancies in history. Nor did Senta feel like facing the stares and sympathy of his lordship's staff. Already this morning her own maid was clucking her tongue. For all Senta knew, the rest of the servants, from the stately butler to the saucy parlor maids, were blaming her for his lordship's sudden flight. Most likely none of them thought she was good enough for their beloved master either.

So Senta escaped to the little family chapel where she had been married just yesterday. The flowers had been removed to the public rooms and the slate floor had been scrubbed after the guests left. No one would bother her here.

It was quite beautiful, besides, with the stained-glass windows letting in a flood of gem-colored light. The thin layer of snow on the ground outside must have magnified the effect, for rainbows patterned the walls and floor and benches. Senta took a seat in a clear crimson sunbeam that streamed through some ancient Morville's robes.

Yesterday she'd been too excited to notice more than the sea of faces, neighbors and family and friends, with retainers standing in the back behind the last filled row of carved wooden pews. After that, she'd only had eyes for her magnificent groom, in his white satin breeches and midnight blue tailed coat. He had a single white rosebud in his lapel, to match the bouquet Senta carried.

She did remember now how the chapel was filled with flowers, their scent everywhere. Someone, Wheatley, she thought, had proudly informed her the blooms were all from the estate's own forcing houses. The man in the back who wept throughout the service must have been the Meadows' gardener. Senta reminded herself to thank him later, to tell him how happy his great sacrifice had made her.

And she had been happy, facing her new life with all the hopes and dreams of innocence. She was going to make Henley Morville the best wife there had ever been. She'd keep his house, entertain his guests, bear his children. She practically had the infants named. There would be no babies now, no chance to make him love her.

"What, are you weeping again? Dang, I hate that."

Senta looked up at the sudden draft and wiped at her eyes. "I thought even the ghosts had deserted me." No such luck.

Sir Parcival was standing in a patch of blue reflected from the stained-glass sky above a cherubic Morville who had died too young. Everything about him was blue, right down to his shoes. As he stepped closer, though, through other colored rays of light, Senta realized he was dressed all in white, with sequins sewn all over his coat. Senta was almost blinded by the rainbows bouncing back from the tiny mirrors. "Are you sure you aren't an angel?"

"I've been called a lot of things in my time, sweetheart, but never that, if I recall."

"No, and you haven't exactly brought me any blessings," she concluded sadly. As a matter of fact, she blamed most of her troubles on this phantom's appearance, but she was too polite to say so. He had enough trouble searching for his missing memory without assuming a burden of guilt for her misery.

On the other hand, he might just be a hallucination and she really was ready for the lunatic asylum. In which case, his feelings wouldn't be hurt. "Oh, go away, do. You've been nothing but a headache."

"Now, *that*, I've been called." He sat next to her, and Senta couldn't resist the urge to touch him, to see if he was real. She nudged her hand along the cushioned seat of the pew, to his sleeve. Her hand passed right through, with a tingling feeling that sent chills up her spine.

"Yeah, it was always like that." He gave her a slow smile that instantly explained to Senta why he always had that effect on the girls.

"So what are you going to do," he was saying, "sit here all day in a river of tears or something?"

"What am I supposed to do, go back to my parents?" Her lip trembling, she waved Maitland's letter, crumpled now and waterlogged. "He doesn't want me."

"Oh, he wants you, all right, sister. A blind man could see that. Of course, he thinks he's too old for you to love him back, but what are twelve years or so? Nah, he's just upset over his brother's death."

"I know. That's why he married me. With his brother gone, he needed an heir."

"No way. He couldn't help falling in love with you. Trust me, I mightn't know my name, but I know about these things. Some loves are just meant to be."

"Thank you." She sniffed into her handkerchief. "But he's still gone."

"So that leaves you to find out what really happened to this brother Michael."

"It was a terrible accident."

"No, that's what they told everyone, but your man knows that just ain't true. He thinks Michael killed himself after making a deal with the enemy that got his own men killed."

"Oh no, not Maitland's brother! I can't believe it."

"But he does. That's what has him chasing his tail like a dog with fleas."

"You mean he's not just angry at me?" Senta permitted a little hope to creep back into her heart.

"He's just trying to protect you, it looks like. Only he's going at it hind end first, begging your pardon, ma'am. Seems there's this old army retiree who might have the real facts, only your boy wouldn't listen. He shut the old guy up in some abandoned cellblock in the woods. We've got to go see the codger and find out what he knows."

"But I can't interfere."

"Well, you can't just sit here, crying in the ... What did you call this place?"

Chapter Five

*W*hat happened to Lord Maitland's sweet and docile bride? If Wheatley the butler was wondering, at least he kept his thoughts to himself. He sent to the stables for the gig—one horse, no groom—as his new mistress had ordered. Her unfamiliarity with the surroundings, the fog settling in over the thin layer of snow, the general unsuitability of Viscountess Maitland going abroad unaccompanied, none of Wheatley's respectful protests were heeded.

"Begging your pardon, my lady, but I am sure the master would not approve."

"Then the master should be here to drive me himself."

Senta got the gig. And she was not going without a companion, for Sir Parcival sat on the bench next to her, directing her to direct the horse, Lulu.

"She was a Christmas present from Lord Maitland," Senta said when Sir Parcival admired the bay mare. "I call her Lou."

"Lou Christmas?"

He really was attics-to-let, her ethereal guest. "No, that's Father Christmas. Goodness, will he be showing up here, too?" He'd be more useful, she thought with just a touch of regret.

They drove up the hill, still within the Meadows' boundaries, and down into the hollow where the viscount maintained a cluster of homes for his tenants and workers. The fog was so bad there, Senta could barely make out the lane to follow.

"It's like pea soup, in the valley."

They had to backtrack a bit on the other side of the valley to find the trail that led through the home woods. At last they reached the clearing.

Senta got down, tied the horse, and said, "This isn't any gaol; it's just a house."

"But the back room has a lock on it."

Sir Parcival followed slowly, his head cocked to one side. "Jailhouse lock?"

Senta picked up a likely-looking rock for smashing the padlock, in case Maitland had taken the key with him.

"Jailhouse stone?" He shook his head. "Nah. That ain't it either."

The key was on a hook beside the door. Private Waters was thrilled to see them, to see Lady Maitland, at least, Sir Parcival being invisible to him.

"Fellow from up at the Meadows brung me food and got the fire going again, but he wouldn't listen to nothing I said about the lieutenant, or Mona, or anything. It was like I didn't exist."

"I can relate to that," Sir Parcival muttered.

"I even tried to slip some coins under the door here, for him to go tell Mona where I'd got to, but he wouldn't touch a groat of it. It's that worrited I am. So if you can just reach me down my wooden leg, I'll say what I come to say and be on my way afore his lordship has a change of heart."

Senta started to say, "His lordship didn't—" but Sir Parcival pinched her. It wasn't exactly a pinch, more a frosty blast, but she got the message. "That is, his lordship truly wants to know what really happened to his brother. Lieutenant Morville could not have been a traitor, could he?"

"Not on your life, my lady, and I'll take on any man who dares say different. He was a good officer, and took right good care of his men. He wouldn't of done nothing to put them in danger, least of all lead them into an ambush."

"And he was loyal to the Crown? He didn't have any Populist leanings?"

"He was an Englishman, ma'am. No offense."

Senta nodded. "Then what happened? How could they accuse him of trafficking with the enemy?"

"Well, I don't know about trafficking, but someone sold the information, that's for sure. We marched right into a company of Frenchies. The lieutenant, he managed to regroup the rear columns and take them around to come behind the Frogs, to save what was left of our troops. He was a regular hero, and none of the men who made it out of there alive could figure why he didn't get a chestful of ribbons. Instead, they shipped him home, quiet like, saying he had an accident."

"But he didn't?"

"The lieutenant could clean and load that rifle in his sleep, ma'am."

"And you don't think he killed himself?"

"No way. He and Mona was going to get married as soon as he could get leave. It was all he talked about. Fellow getting legshackled don't up and shoot hisself."

Senta thought of Lord Maitland and wondered if that was true. If he was desperate enough to end a marriage ... "You say Lieutenant Morville loved this Mona?"

"As God is my witness. And then there was the Frenchy blunt they found in his billet. Well, it wasn't there in the morning when I made up the bunk. They made me swear not to talk about it ... and then they made sure I was shipped off so I couldn't ask any more questions."

"So what do you think happened?" Senta asked.

Waters scratched his bald head. "Well, some turncoat gave away our position, that's a pure fact. Then the rat framed Lieutenant Morville."

"And . . . killed him?"

"He would of defended hisself, otherwise. Dead heroes don't tell no tales. There were two fine London gents in camp the week of the battle, gambling and drinking with all the officers. My guess is one or both of them was the traitor. Now they're out to blackmail Lord Maitland, on account of the brass letting him claim an accident with the gun."

"Is that why Lord Maitland went to London, because someone was blackmailing him?" No wonder he was distracted!

Private Waters eyed her narrowly. "Didn't he tell you what he was doing?"

"He, ah, didn't want to worry me."

"Well, you best worry. Iffen I miss my guess, one of those lying, cheating toffs is a murderer asides."

Dear heaven, Lee was in danger! Senta looked toward Sir Parcival for help, but he was combing his hair in the little washstand mirror.

"Do you have any proof? Do you know their names? Their direction?"

"No, but Mona saw them and heard them talking about someone named Antoine. That's a Frenchy name for sure. She was serving in the cantina at the time, and they didn't know she could speak English. Don't go thinking Mona's just a tavern wench, like the colonel said, when she went to him with her suspicions. She was a right proper lady, but the war killed her family and she had to make her own way. She was working there just until she and the lieutenant could get hitched, so as they could have proper digs, not a tent in a muddy field."

"I see, I think. But Mona doesn't know the men's names? Can she recognize them?"

"She could of, if his high-and-mighty lordship hadn't gone off in a rant, begging your pardon, ma'am. Now he's liable to stir up a real hornet's nest, leading right back to Mona and me. So I'll just go fetch her from that inn in your village, and we'll be on our way."

Private Waters quickly learned that Lady Maitland was nearly as hardheaded as her husband. She didn't lock him up, but she took his wooden leg with her in the gig, to go fetch Mona.

"Then we'll find you a safe place to stay until his lordship gets back and can listen."

Waters spit out the door. "And pigs'll fly."

Mona was happy to leave the inn with Senta once she saw the peg leg. She'd been nervous there by herself, even with Private Waters's wallet and pistol. She pulled the latter out of her wide black skirts, to Senta's discomfort. In her imperfect English she made it quite plain that she would do anything she could to clear her lost love's name and hold his murderers to account.

"I, Ramona Consuela las Flores y Vegas, I shall tear their hearts out with my bare hands," the small, dark-haired woman swore, "the way they stole my *corazón*." Then she started to cry.

"Another weeping willow," complained Sir Parcival. "Man, I can't stand this." He tried to put his arms around her. "That's all right, Mona." His arms went right through her, and she kept crying and shivering, until Senta suggested she go upstairs and gather her belongings.

When Mona returned, she wasn't carrying bags and boxes; she had a baby in her arms.

Oh Lud, Senta was thinking, and the private said she was a lady. Lord Maitland wasn't going to be happy about this. Wheatley wasn't going to be happy about this. Her own mother would have kitten fits, if she ever found out. Senta turned to Sir Parcival for some guidance. He was as happy as a grig, entranced by the infant who was gurgling up at him and reaching for his gold necklace. The babe seemed confused when her little hands couldn't touch the glittery object. Senta was confused, too.

Sir Parcival shrugged. "It's a female thing. And innocence."

Innocence, which seemed to be in short suppy on the Peninsula.

Mona raised her chin. "We were, *cómo se dice*, promised? We were going to be married, my Miguel and I." Shifting the baby to her shoulder, Mona reached into the bodice of her heavy black dress. She pulled out a chain. "Miguel, he said, '*Cara*, until we can wed, wear my ring around your neck.' "

Senta recognized the Maitland family crest on the gold ring, a match to the one her husband wore constantly. Michael would not have parted lightly with his. Sir Parcival nodded.

Mona tucked the chain back out of sight. "But to wait, with the battles, the danger . . ." She shrugged. "Things are different with the army."

"You can say that again, ma'am."

The Spanish girl turned the baby in her arms. "He never got to see his daughter, but Miguel, he would have loved her very much. I named her Vida, for life. Vida Miguela las Flores y Vegas."

"Vida las Flores? Vida las Vegas? Man, that almost sounds familiar."

Mona smiled tenderly at the infant, while Senta scowled at Sir Parcival for fussing with his lost memory now. Unfortunately, Mona caught Senta's look of disgust. She stared back defiantly. "If you cannot accept my *niña*, me and my Miguel's love child, I will understand. This is not the thing for grand señoras, this I know. We can wait here for Private Waters. He is a good friend."

"I'm sure he is, but my husband will want to make provision for his brother's child." Senta crossed her fingers behind her back. Maitland was so very proper. He already believed Mona was a mere camp follower. Heaven knew what he'd think if she sprang a baby from the wrong side of the blanket on him. "Besides, until we find the real traitors, you are not safe here alone."

"But I am not alone. Private Waters left his dog here to guard me and Vida." She handed the infant to Senta and went to fetch the animal.

"I had a dog once," Sir Parcival reminisced while Senta jiggled the baby. "I'm sure of it."

"Will you forget about remembering what you forgot!" Senta hissed. "We have to figure what to do with all of them."

An old brindle bitch plodded at Mona's side. "Her name is Sheba," Mona told them.

"Old Sheba? Nah, that wasn't it."

There was a problem when they returned to fetch Private Waters. Senta had thought getting Maitland to accept Mona and Vida, and listen to Private Waters, was her big hurdle. She didn't even consider what she was going to tell the staff at the Meadows to explain the unlikely trio. Quartet if you included Sheba, who was nothing like the sleek, well-fed foxhounds in his lordship's kennels.

That wasn't the problem, however. After a hurried conversation with the old soldier in Spanish, Mona refused to go to the Meadows.

"*Su esposo*, your husband, he believes my Miguel was a traitor."

"That's what the army told him. We have to help him prove otherwise. That's why you came, isn't it?"

"He called me *puta*. I will not sleep under his roof. We will stay here, in this little house."

Senta didn't bother saying that the cottage was as much Maitland's as the Meadows was. "But the man he sent to guard Private Waters will be back. He'll lock him up and toss you out."

Mona was adamant. "Me, I have slept on the ground before. We will camp in this forest until he begs my forgiveness, your so proud viscount."

"But it's cold!" Senta feared it might be a cold day in hell before Maitland took in a baseborn child and its unwed mother. "And you must think of the baby! January in England is not what you are used to in Spain."

Private Waters scratched at his chin. "She's right, and there are game wardens prowling about, and poachers, too. It ain't safe. We can't go back to that inn neither; the keep's wife weren't none too keen on babies, or foreigners, or young girls with no wedding ring, even if I did say you was my daughter-in-law. And getting hauled out of there oncet was enough, thankee."

Senta did some quick thinking. "I know. There used to be a hermit living in a cave by the ornamental lake. It was all the rage in Lord Maitland's mother's time, he told me. But they couldn't get anyone to take the position, to look picturesque, you know, until they built a snug dwelling at the back of the cave, with a fireplace and all. It's still habitable. His lordship took me there before Christmas."

Senta pretended to fuss with the baby's blanket, to hide her blushes. They were supposed to be gathering holly and ivy to decorate the hall under the watchful chaperonage of Mama, two cousins, and an old aunt. Instead, the viscount had tugged her inside the cave for a quick kiss, their first.

"No one goes near there in winter, and it's close enough to the house that I can come visit and bring whatever you need, just until Lord Maitland gets home and straightens everything out. You'll be warm and safe from prying eyes in the grotto."

Sir Parcival looked up from making the baby coo with his humming. "In the grotto? You're going to stash them in the grotto?"

* * *

Now all Senta had to do was explain to Wheatley how the footman's visits to the cottage in the forest were no longer necessary. She did not want the stable hands and gardeners scouring the home woods for a one-legged soldier.

"About that small difficulty at the gamekeeper's cottage," Senta informed Wheatley, trying her hardest to imitate Lady Drummond-Burrell's haughtiest tones. "I have taken care of matters myself."

"And that troublesome report of a young foreign person in the village, with an infant?"

Lud, nothing got past Wheatley. "I have seen to that also. They have all left the countryside."

Wheatley was relieved. Such havey-cavey goings-on at the cottage were not what he was used to, and that other situation boded no good for anyone. With no directions from Lord Maitland, Wheatley had been at a stand: leave the young person in the village to generate heaven knew what rumors or insults, or incarcerate her with that other fellow, quite illegally. Let the young mistress deal with it. Lord Maitland would never have her pretty young head on a platter.

"I am going to want some baskets of food," Senta told him, so he could notify the kitchens. "I noticed some of the tenants appeared to be in need."

Wheatley nodded, as if Lord Maitland would ever let any of his people go hungry. He'd guess she had the ragtag group in the boathouse or the grotto. He'd have to warn the staff to keep their distance. Welladay, she'd make a viscountess yet.

So Senta saw her guests settled in, and sat back to wait for Lord Maitland's return so she could surprise him with proof that his brother wasn't a loose screw, just a tad impatient. What a surprise that would be! She waited for him, and waited . . . and cried herself to sleep.

Sir Parcival walked the halls of the Meadows night after night, echoes of Senta's fallen teardrops jumbled in his head with all the confusion of places, people, poetry. He had no one to talk to when Senta slept. Out in the grotto the baby would gurgle for him, but she wasn't much of a conversationalist, and her mama cried. He had no way to make things right for her, either. He was no closer to promoting anyone's happiness or regaining his own memory.

With heavy heart, Sir Parcival went back to the slumbering soul in the suit of armor in the entry hall. "Are you lonesome too, knight?"

Chapter Six

$\mathcal{L}$ord Maitland did not come home that week. He was not going to come home the following week. Senta knew it in her heart, the same as she knew that if she wanted to save her marriage, she had to go to London. He couldn't very well claim irreconcilable differences if they were living in the same house, could he? On the other hand, he would be so furious that she'd followed him to Town like a lost puppy that he might pack her up, bag and baggage, and ship her to her parents in Yorkshire, or some one of his far-flung holdings. Then she'd never get to prove to him that she hadn't married him for his wealth and title.

But if she did travel to London, Lord Maitland might think she merely craved the parties and entertainments of Town life, that she couldn't be content in the country. He'd think she'd spun her love of the rural life out of whole cloth, just to meet his requirements in a bride. When she'd told him how much she enjoyed small-town living and bucolic pastimes like riding and gardening and observing nature, she hadn't meant all by herself!

She also recalled blushing when the viscount had asked if she liked children. What did it matter that she adored babies, if she was never to have one of her own? Tiny Vida was precious, but she was Mona's baby. Maitland wasn't about to beget his heir by wishful thinking . . . if he still considered Senta a fit mother to his children. How could she stand his telling her not, face-to-face? No, she'd better wait here and hope he came to his senses. Perhaps a letter?

But there was the problem of his brother's death. Lee hadn't taken Senta into his confidence, which the meanest intelligence could assume meant that he wouldn't like her knowing about the accident/suicide, much less her putting her nose into his affairs. But if it was murder, then he had to know. Senta couldn't bear sitting over her embroidery while her husband's life might be in danger.

Besides, everyone for miles must already know about Mona and the baby, with all the supplies Senta had been toting out to the grotto. She'd even raided the attic for infant clothes and a small cradle. Wheatley and his staff were very good about turning their backs when she piled load after load onto the gig, but they must know. And Private Waters's dog begged at the kitchen door no matter how many scraps Senta put into the baskets of food. So their presence was no secret, and they could be in danger, too. In London, Mona could dress up as a lady's maid so she wouldn't be recognized as a foreigner. No one noticed servants or spoke to them anyway. And in London they could all help in the investigation into Michael's death.

But Senta had promised to obey her husband. He hadn't exactly ordered her to stay put, but he'd meant it. He wanted to be in London alone, to see about the blackmailers, and his business interests, and his Parliament responsibilities . . . and his old flirts. Senta had to go.

She put it to Sir Parcival. "Should I go to London or stay here?"

"Did I ever play there?" he wanted to know.

"How should I know where you played? I don't even know what century you lived!" Today Sir Parcival was dressed in a loose plaid jacket, but she could not identify the tartan. His trousers were somewhat in the cossack style, with extra fabric everywhere. No, she doubted he'd set out after the Holy Grail in that outfit. His feelings were obviously hurt, so she added, "That is, many little boys sail their boats on the Serpentine, so it's possible. I know they love to visit Astley's Amphitheatre and the menagerie at the Tower. My little cousins were in alt when they visited last spring. They rolled their hoops in Grosvenor Square for hours. Does any of that sound familiar?"

"Just the square part."

"But shall I go? Would it be a ninnyish thing to do?"

He listened carefully to all her reasoning, pro and con, then said, "Well, wise men say . . ."

"Yes? What do they say?" Perhaps her gudgeon of a ghost really knew some wiser heads.

"I can't remember."

Senta decided to go. Then she had to convince her entourage.

"I ain't going." Private Waters crossed his arms over his scrawny chest. "The man'd as soon send me to the Antipodes as give me the time of day. He wouldn't listen afore; he ain't going to listen now."

"But he won't have to listen to you. That is, he'll have to listen to me. I'll explain the whole thing, you'll see. And you never meant to extort money from him, so he really cannot charge you with anything. I rather think he'll be grateful to you"—and to herself—"for bringing this matter to his attention."

She prayed it was so. She needed Private Waters with her as her excuse for coming to London in the first place. The evidence she could present, showing that his brother was a loyal officer, ought to outweigh Maitland's anger at her presence. *Ought* was the pivotal word here. Senta couldn't begin to fathom the viscount's mind.

"What'll I do there? Can't go on living on his charity, especially how his lordship thinks I crawled out from under a rock, just to queer his game."

"You won't be dependent on his goodwill at all, Mr. Waters. I have an enormous household account and a generous allowance." She wanted this old soldier to think better of her husband, so she added, "Lord Maitland really is quite open-handed."

Waters's only comment was to spit between the gap in his teeth. Senta stepped back. "Yes, well, I can pay your wages myself. You can be my personal footman."

"You having a footman with one foot, tagging behind carrying your parcels and delivering your notes, is sure to sit fine with his high-and-mighty lordship. I'll do it."

Mona wasn't as easy to convince. London, in that *perro* Maitland's house? Never. Besides, it wasn't fitting for Lady Maitland to have an unwed mother in her home. She knew how things were in the *beau monde*. Mona was grateful enough for this time to rest from the journey; she would not ruin Senta's good name.

Senta's name would be mud if Maitland went through with the annulment, but she was not about to discuss that with Mona. Instead she reasoned that no one would have to know. They would simply call her a widow, Señora Vegas, who was acting as Lady Maitland's companion. That way Mona could go about with Senta in society, looking for the two men who played cards with Michael Morville, then framed him for treason and killed him.

"It's the only way we are going to clear Michael's name," Senta told her. "And think of the baby. You can't keep little Vida living in a cave, for heaven's sake!"

"But you will tell your husband who we are?"

"Of course. He has to know, in order to make his investigation, and to make some arrangement for your future. I know you are proud, and I know you would do your best to find work, but again, what about the baby? That kind of life is not what Michael would have intended for his child. Further, you would be dishonoring his memory, making him into a libertine who used women in the basest manner without taking responsibility for the outcome."

"Not my Miguel! Never!"

"Then let his brother fulfil Michael's obligations. Let Maitland look after you and Vida. It's the only way."

Mona nodded. "But what if this grand nobleman of yours rejects us? What if he says Miguel would never have promised to marry so far beneath him? What if he does not believe my precious *hija* is Miguel's baby at all?"

"Then you and Vida and Private Waters, if he wishes, will always have a home at my parents' house in Yorkshire. With me."

That left Wheatley to win over.

"But, my lady, his lordship left very specific instructions that you were to remain here until his return."

"Were those my husband's only instructions?" Senta asked in her sweetest tones.

"No, my lady," poor Wheatley had to confess, having said as much to Lady Maitland when she was first abandoned here. He'd been trying to make the master seem less of a blackguard, more fool he. "The master directed the staff to see that you had everything you wanted."

"Thank you, Wheatley. I want to go to London."

"But Maitland House is not up to our standards at this time. His lordship uses only a small portion of the rooms. The rest are in Holland covers or a state of deterioration."

"I've driven past Lord Maitland's London residence.

The outside is quite grand. Do you mean to tell me that it is a hovel inside?"

The butler cleared his throat. "Not precisely. The late viscountess did not often visit the city once she started filling her nursery. Her husband, the previous Lord Maitland, took no interest in domestic affairs like seat covers and wall hangings, less so when his lady passed on. His lordship, the current viscount, also prefers the Meadows as his residence; he frequently patronizes his clubs when in the city, so never saw the need to refurbish the town house. Therefore, the Portman Square property has been without a woman's touch for a long while."

"Too long. That's all the more reason for me to go, don't you agree? Someone should see about restoring the place to its former glory, to do the family name proud. Why, his lordship is very involved in governmental affairs. How can he entertain his political friends in a ramshackle old barn of a place?"

Wheatley took a deep breath. "But there is almost no staff to speak of: his lordship's man, the cook-housekeeper, a few maids, and perhaps two footmen. Not nearly enough to see Maitland House set to rights. I could send a staff ahead to ready it for your ladyship's arrival if you wish."

And warn the viscount so he could forbid her to come. "I'm sure a few days of discomfort without an army of servants around will not give me a disgust of the place. And they do have employment agencies in London, you know."

The butler blotted beads of perspiration from his forehead. "Take on strangers at Maitland House?"

"No? Then you'll come, too?"

Wheatley made one last try: "But his lordship had important business to transact in London. He will not appreciate the commotion of moving the household or renovating the premises."

"Oh, we shan't interfere with his lordship's business

at all. We'll be so quiet, he won't even know we are there."

Senta was to ride in the crested carriage with her maid, led by outriders and postilions. A hired coach for Mona and her baby, Private Waters, his dog, and the new nursemaid followed. Another three carriages were required for the staff Wheatley insisted they needed. One fourgon held Senta's trousseau. She'd bought the gowns, bonnets, and negligees for Lord Maitland to see; by heaven, he was going to see them. Of course, she could buy new clothes while in London, but Senta was determined to look fashionable while shopping, at least as fashionable as the demireps who would be hanging on her husband's sleeve. Senta was *not* some dowdy matron come up from the country; she'd had two London Seasons and meant to look the part. Maitland would have nothing to complain about in her appearance.

Another coach held the china and linens Wheatley deemed necessary for civilized living, until the house was in order. Three wagons were following with enough produce from their own farms to feed an army on the march. Hams, chickens, mutton, smoked fish, sacks of vegetables, flour from the local mill, cheeses from the dairy, oranges from the conservatory, carefully preserved herbs, and Cook's special spices. London could not provide anything near the quality of their own harvest. Cook had a carriage of his own, with his precious pots and pans.

"I thought you didn't want to draw any attention," Sir Parcival commented with that half sneer as they got ready to leave. "How you're going to keep sixteen coaches a secret is a mystery to me."

Senta looked over the crowded courtyard. "I count eleven."

She couldn't worry over her addled apparition. Not today. Today she was going to London, to her husband.

She got in the lead coach, leaving Sir Parcival shaking his head. He hunched his shoulders. "Then again, life's a train of mysteries to me these days."

Chapter Seven

"*B*loody hell!"

Lord Maitland was drawn to the entry of his Portman Square residence by the sounds of commotion in the street. Only the commotion was not in the street, it was in his own hallway. Now he stood in his shirtsleeves, as his previously tranquil household was turned into a circus. There were footmen performing acrobatics with trunks, maids juggling parcels. There was even an animal act, an old dog most likely with a flea circus of its own.

"What the deuce?"

His cook, his own personal chef, whom he'd ransomed out of a prison ship, was shouting hysterically at a squad of helpers. He was shouting in French, naturally, which not a one of them understood. "Do not excite yourself over the unpacking, Jacques," Lee told the man, "for you'll be returning to the Meadows on the instant."

"Non, non, monsieur, the food, it must be unloading before it spoils. Ice, I need ice," he shouted. *"Tout de suite."*

Amid the turmoil Lee's butler was issuing orders, directing traffic, overseeing the unloading of an entire caravan of coaches parked up and down the street. The neighbors must be getting an eyeful.

"You don't have to worry about the foodstuffs," Lee told the cook in a controlled fury, "for you'll be serving Wheatley's liver and lights unless this whole mingle-mangle is straighted out and you are on your way back to the Meadows within the hour."

Wheatley bowed. "I am sorry, my lord, but that will be impossible, with all due respect. The horses are tired, for one, and the staff at the Meadows has been given a holiday while the premises are being treated with a solution of turpentine and a bit of arsenic. Termites, my lord, I regret to say."

"Termites!" Lee exploded. "There are no termites at the Meadows! Who gave that bloody order?"

"Why, I did, of course," Senta told him in her most dulcet tones, hoping her voice wouldn't quaver and betray that she was shaking in her half boots. She took her hand out of her ermine muff and held it toward him.

In front of the hordes of servants there was nothing Lee could do but bow over the offered hand and kiss her fingers. "Lady Maitland, what a pleasant surprise." Under his breath, he muttered, "You better have a deuced good explanation for this."

He'd never looked so dear to Senta, with his shirt collar open and his sandy hair mussed, nor so intimidating. She wanted to throw herself into his arms and beg him to let her stay, but that wasn't the way to win him over, she knew. She had to prove her loyalty. Well, she shouldn't *have* to, she thought with a twinge of resentment. She was his wife, by all the saints. Still, given his unfortunate opinion of her, she had to earn his trust. Of course, disobeying his orders wasn't the best way to start.

She pretended to survey the hallway while the servants swirled around them. Wheatley was right: the hangings were dingy, the wood railings were dull, the carpets were faded underfoot and threadbare in places.

159

"It's a good thing I arrived when I did. This place certainly needs a woman's touch."

"You are not staying," he uttered through clenched teeth. She could see the muscles of his jaw spasm.

Just then another long line of footmen, all in Maitland's blue-and-gold livery, entered the hall. One short fellow was hidden behind a tall pile of parcels, but there was no hiding the man's wooden leg.

"What the devil?"

"Oh, we knew how you wanted to keep an eye on the man, so we brought him along."

Keep an eye on him? Lee wanted the fellow bound and gagged. He started forward, but felt an arm at his elbow.

"He's given his parole not to escape, and really, you'll find him quite useful."

Lee was about to tell her how he could use the old trooper as bait when he went fishing next, when a woman entered through the open doors. She was dressed in black from head to toe, with a veil hiding her face, so all Lee could tell was that she was of average height. She curtsied in his direction, then followed a maid up the stairs.

"Who the blazes was that?"

"Oh, that was my new companion," Senta gaily replied. "You wouldn't want me traveling alone, would you? It's not at all the thing."

He didn't want her traveling, period, but before he could utter the words, a maid in a gray uniform with a gray cape entered, with a blanket-draped bundle in her arms. Wheatley had a footman escort her above.

"And that? That . . . ?"

"We'll discuss that later, my lord, when you're feeling more the thing."

"We'll talk about it now." He took her arm in a none-too-gentle hold and half dragged Senta down the hall.

She could only be glad he hadn't seen Sir Parcival, who'd gotten hold of a medieval lute somewhere in the ether and was trying to fix its strings. He was dressed today in some iridescent silver suit, with ruffles on his shirt collar. And his legs were twitching.

"What's wrong with you?" she mouthed at him behind Lee's back. Did ghosts get rabies?

"Well, bless my soul," he replied with a wink, kissing the instrument. "I'm in love." He disappeared through the wall, leaving Senta feeling somewhat bereft, somewhat relieved.

And more than somewhat nervous as she faced her angry husband in his library. She was pleased to see that this room, at least, was in excellent repair, with a fire going in the grate. She started toward the warming flames, but her husband took her arm again and swung her to face him.

"What is the meaning of this, madam?" he shouted. "Don't you know this will make it twice as hard to get an annulment?"

Of course she knew. Senta's heart rejoiced that he hadn't seen the deed done already.

Just then someone cleared his throat. They both turned to find Mr. Calley, his lordship's secretary, standing red-faced behind his desk.

Senta nodded to him, having met the man when he came to the Meadows to help with the wedding arrangements. He was quite the tallest man of her acquaintance, taller than the viscount, taller than Sir Parcival, who had entered the room through the ceiling and was studying the secretary's long frame. He was wearing that remembering look Senta was beginning to know quite well, half-hopeful, half-confused. Trying to see if a name could jar his memory, Senta began, "Good day to you, Mr. Cal—"

But his lordship interrupted. "That will be all for today, John."

"Very well, my lord, Lady Maitland. And may I take this opportunity to welcome you to—"

161

"No, you may not. Her ladyship is not staying. You are excused, John."

Senta had taken the opportunity to remove her fur-lined cloak and seat herself near the fire. Let the viscount shout across the room if he wanted; Senta was not going to budge.

To which end she informed her husband, "I am not leaving."

Lee took three deep breaths to calm himself. Then he started pacing. "What happened to the sweet young thing I married? In two weeks you've turned into the most hardheaded of women."

Sir Parcival's legs started having tics again. Senta couldn't watch the poor man's palsy anymore. She turned back to her husband in time to hear: "I could have you picked up and carried home bodily, you know. A wife is a husband's property, to do with as he will. But I am not a tyrant. If you are so determined to be here, say your piece now, before I move to one of my clubs."

"What, and make a laughingstock of both of us? Is that why you married me?"

Things were bad enough already, Lee knew. He was well aware that they were the butt of every kind of malicious gossip going the rounds. The bridegroom appearing in London within days of his wedding, sans bride, was a natural target for conjecture, if not outright insult. As a matter of fact, he had not been going to his clubs for that very reason. Nor Gentleman Jackson's Boxing Parlor, Manton's Gallery, or any other of his usual haunts. He hadn't brought himself to seek out his solicitor yet either.

So he wouldn't move out. Rather than concede, however, he growled, "That's better than why you married me, I swear."

Senta wanted to tell him that she'd married him because she loved him and wanted desperately to make

162

him love her. Instead she quietly told him, "I married you because I thought we could be happy together."

Lee ran his fingers through his hair. "Well, now you can see that we don't suit. You'd be better out of the marriage."

The best offense being a good defense, Senta went on the attack. "You wouldn't betray your country, would you?"

"Of course not. What's that to the purpose?"

"The purpose is that your brother would no more commit treason than you would!"

"My brother? What do you know about my brother? Oh, you've been talking to the old gaffer with the wooden leg."

"No, I've been listening to Private Waters. There's a difference, you know."

"And what did that mawworm try to get out of you, to insure his silence?"

"All he wants is to clear your brother's name, my lord. Why can you not accept that?"

Lee turned from his pacing and pounded his fist into the mantel. "Because it's impossible, that's why. Dash it, do you think I could accept that my brother was a traitor without proof? They showed me, his general, his field officer, his major, the colonel who treated Michael like his own son. The man had tears in his eyes, by Jupiter."

Sir Parcival had tears in his eyes now, too.

"But what if they were wrong?" Senta asked quietly.

"If they were wrong, then Michael would be alive."

"Unless someone killed him in such a fashion to make him look more guilty."

"Killed him? You and that . . . relic have concocted a murder out of this?" He finally took a seat in the chair facing Senta's, with his head thrown back.

"Would you rather believe your brother was a traitor or a murder victim?"

For the first time, Lee began to doubt what he'd been

given as truth. "Do you have proof? Damn, just a shred of evidence would give me hope."

"You'll have to speak to Private Waters for yourself. I was convinced, I admit."

"And that's what brought you to London?"

Senta didn't answer. She just asked how far he'd gotten with his search for the two wellborn civilians who were at army headquarters at the right time, who won Michael's gambling chits the night before the ambush.

"Half the War Office staff is away on holiday still, but I've managed to get a list of what wounded officers were sent home on leave that sennight. I have men making inquiries as to how they were transported, who met them, et cetera."

"If they were Londoners, Mona could recognize them for you."

"Mona? Wasn't Mona the name of Waters's Spanish, ah, convenient? Please tell me that the woman who entered my house dressed in black, your new companion, is not a common camp follower."

"She was no such thing. She was Michael's fiancée."

Now he reached across the space between their chairs and took her hands in his. "Senta, you have a kind heart, but people will tell you what they want you to believe. That doesn't make it so. Michael would have written to me if he was betrothed."

Squeezing his hand, trying to make him see, Senta asked, "Would you have approved? Was Michael a frequent correspondent? Were the mails from Portugal always reliable?"

"No. No. And no. But that doesn't prove this female even knew Michael. She and Waters could have cobbled this hubble-bubble for your sake. They want your sympathy, don't you see, so you will come down heavy with conscience money. Or convince me to."

Senta touched the heavy gold signet ring that never left his hand. "She has Michael's ring. And no, don't even think of saying that she could have stolen it. According to Private Waters, some of the evidence against Michael was that he was found with a great deal of money. That would have been easier to take, easier to get rid of, than his distinctive ring. I really believe she loved your brother. She wants to help find his murderer." Reluctantly she removed her hands from his. "We all want to help."

"What, get another female involved in this? Never. It was bad enough trying to shield you from possible scandal, Senta, but now . . . If there really is a murderer loose, I don't want you or any other woman anywhere near. No, you and your, ah, companion are going home in the morning." Lud, how could he keep her here, when just the touch of her hand had him yearning to make her his?

"Without anyone to protect us? You wouldn't."

Deuce take it, he wouldn't. He couldn't let her go again. Bad enough there were highwaymen and bands of unemployed soldiers on the roads, now he'd have to worry about murderous traitors, too. Besides, he could see that Senta was struggling to hide her yawns and drooping eyelids. The journey must have been wearisome. "We'll speak of this again in a day or two, when you have rested."

That was more than she'd hoped for. Senta hurried to her feet before he could mention the two words she wanted least to hear.

"But this changes nothing between us, you know. I still intend to seek an annulment."

There was one of them.

"Oh, and perhaps you might spare me a last moment to explain that other item you thought we'd discuss later."

"Item? I don't recall anything else that we needed to discuss, as long as you agree to speak to Private Waters and Mona." She scurried toward the door, knowing that a footman would be on the other side waiting to show her to her room, where she'd be safe. If Lord Maitland was going to have the marriage set aside, he certainly was not going to be visiting her this evening.

"The baby, Senta."

There was the second word. "The, ah, baby?" She turned at the door and took a deep breath. "The baby. Yes, well, she has your smile. When you smile, that is."

"What?" Lee bellowed. He was not smiling now. "Are you accusing me of leaving my butter stamp around the countryside?"

"Of course not. That is, I hope you shan't be bringing baseborn children home, except if you do not intend to make our marriage a true one, and you still wish heirs, I suppose—"

"Senta!"

"Very well. She is Mona's baby, and Michael's. The sweetest, dearest infant you can imagine. Her name is Vida."

Lee shook his head. "You did say fiancée, didn't you, in reference to Michael's inamorata? Not wife?"

"These things happen, my lord."

"Oh, I am well aware that they happen. They just don't usually happen in noble households in the middle of London, where gossip is as pervasive as the fog. Your so-called companion is no better than she ought to be, and her child is a bastard."

"And your niece."

He ignored that for now. "Just what kind of acceptance do you think you'll find in London, or anywhere in the whole country for that matter, if it's spread about that you associate with soiled doves and their illegitimate offspring?"

"About as friendly a reception, my lord, as I would get if your brother is named a traitor, which he might be without Mona's help. And as cordial a greeting as I would receive if you cast me aside like an old shoe. Good night, my lord."

With that, she made good her exit, before her husband could issue any orders.

"Bloody hell," Lee muttered to himself as he poured a glass of brandy. "Does a man ever win one of these arguments?"

"Once in a blue moon," Sir Parcival answered. "Once in a blue, blue moon."

Chapter Eight

It was even more important to find the blackmailer now, Lord Maitland thought. If there really was a murder, then the blackhearted extortionist might lead him to Michael's killer. He might even *be* Michael's killer, so confident that he'd gotten away with his heinous crime. Lee *would* find him, and make him pay.

But it made no difference, he thought, sitting by the fire, whether Michael was exposed as a traitor or exonerated as a victim of foul play. Senta would still be better off with the man of her dreams.

The man of her dreams—fuddled nightmare, more like—was having girl trouble of his own. Sir Parcival was in the nursery playing with little Vida, but she wanted to be picked up. The infant could not understand why her friend with all the glittery rings and gemstudded belts would not lift her out of the prison of her cradle.

"I'd rock you if I could, buttercup, all night long," he told the unhappy child, "but my rocking won't work any better'n my memory. Now, roll over and go to sleep."

Instead, Vida started crying. She set up such a racket that the nursemaid was there, Mona was there, and Private Waters was there with his pistol and his dog. But the baby didn't need a clean nappy, a midnight snack, or protecting. She wanted Sir Parcival, now.

The wailing got louder. Senta arrived and took her hand at cuddling, patting, walking the halls with Vida, for Mona was exhausted from their trip. The nursemaid decided Vida was teething, and went off to find the coral ring somewhere in their unpacked baggage.

Still Vida screamed, turning all red and overheated. Now Sheba added her howls. Senta kept walking, Sir Parcival kept dangling shiny things in front of her, but Vida wasn't falling for that trick again. There was never anything there when she reached out, nothing to clasp, nothing to chew on, only cold air. She screamed some more.

"What the devil is going on?" Lord Maitland demanded from the doorway.

Private Waters swung his pistol around, in the viscount's direction. Sheba growled.

"Oh, put that away, old man, before you shoot someone by accident. And tell your mutt that this is *my* home. It seems I may owe you an apology. We'll talk in the morning." When Waters still didn't lower the weapon, Lee told him, "But don't think that means I've decided to keep you on, you insolent antique."

"Nor I ain't decided I want to be in the employ of anyone so hot to hand." But the gun was tucked in the waistband of Waters's trousers.

"Fair enough. But what did you think I was going to do anyway, run amok among all these women and children?" There seemed to be only one child, but the noise level was such that Lee wondered if his wife had any other surprises tucked in the old nursery's odd corners. There were any number of ill-gotten children and stray dogs in the streets of London for her to drag home.

The females were eyeing him suspiciously, except the infant, who was howling like a banshee. Lee nodded to the nursemaid, then bowed slightly to the dark-haired woman who was still dressed in black, although some of the gown's buttons were undone, as if she'd dressed hurriedly. "Welcome to my home, doña. I share your grief."

Mona nodded, but did not say anything. She was just too tired to fight with this toplofty aristocrat, and she was too embarrassed that her child was creating such a fuss in his house.

Lee bent his head toward where Senta was still jiggling the infant, to no avail. "May I?"

Mona bit her lip but gave her permission, since he'd asked so politely. Senta carefully transferred the furious bundle into his arms. Lee held the squalling infant gingerly at first, as if she were made of spun sugar that could crumple at his lightest touch. "So much noise from such a small person." He tried to keep the child's hands from thrashing around. "There, there, little one, shush." Vida didn't shush. Sheba started howling again.

"Thunderation!" Lee was about to hand the child back. Lud, his head was aching from the caterwauling. Besides, this scrap was nothing to him. He could tell. There was no resemblance in this dark-haired, dark-eyed foreigner, no bond, no affection. He felt nothing for her but the urge to have her gone. And quiet.

Then Lee reached into his pocket for his fob watch and dangled it in front of the baby's eyes.

Now, this was more like it! The watch hand moved, the casing glittered, the chain was a fascinating pattern, and the whole thing ticked loudly! Vida stopped screeching and reached for the watch, her tiny brows furrowed in concentration to see if this new toy would slip through her fingers. It didn't. She hiccuped and tried to put it in her mouth. Three women came running, but Lee said, "It's only a watch." And it had only been in his family for generations.

Then Sir Parcival started singing, some "Hey Nonny Nonny" air from the parlor maids. Vida spat out the watch, keeping it firmly in her little fists, and she grinned. If the direction of Vida's gummy grin was somewhere over Lord Maitland's right shoulder, he never noticed.

"You're right," he told Senta. "That's Michael's smile. He was always laughing. And thank you," he said to Mona, even begrudgingly jerking his head toward Private Waters, "for bringing my niece home."

There was no more talk of sending them all back to the Meadows. There were five new footmen and armed guards whenever Senta and Mona were abroad, which was often. Senta was determined to establish herself as Lee's wife in society, to make it harder for the viscount to discard her. So she accepted invitations, paid morning visits, and held at-homes. Mona was equally determined to help unmask the criminals, so she entrusted Vida to the nursemaid and trailed Lady Maitland's skirts, keeping a watchful eye for familiar faces, from behind her black veil.

Senta also decided to make herself indispensable to her husband. He wouldn't come to her bedchamber, and she couldn't go to his uninvited, but she could certainly make his home a more pleasant place. She threw herself into refurbishing Maitland House with a zeal that could have gotten Hannibal's elephants back across those mountains, twice.

Surprisingly, Sir Parcival was a big help, better than Mona, to whom the English styles were overstuffed and overcrowded. Sir Parcival, on the other hand, liked everything and thought she should have it all.

"See? This parlor looks empty and bare. Needs more chairs."

"Yes, and I can hang a picture right . . . over the mantel."

When in doubt, Senta asked the viscount, then she took Wheatley's advice.

* * *

Town was beginning to fill as the ton trickled back, especially the more conscientious members of Parliament and their wives. There were no grand parties as yet where Senta felt the chances of Mona recognizing anyone were better, but there were the theater and the opera.

One night toward the end of January, they sat in the Maitland box, Mona to Senta's left, with her opera glasses scanning the audience. Senta was wearing her diamonds and a new gown of silver tulle over a satin underskirt, with brilliants strewn across the bodice. She caught her husband's frequent bemused glances. No, the décolletage wasn't too low, as she'd feared. It was just right. For tonight she would be content to bask in his clear admiration, even if he wouldn't let her any closer. For tonight she could imagine herself happily married, and escorted by the two most handsome men in all of London. So what if one of them was invisible to everyone else? He liked her dress, too.

Lee was not happy with this evening. His wife was exposing herself to danger. Hell, another half inch and she'd be exposing herself altogether. But she seemed so happy. Even Mona, whom they were calling Señora Vegas, looked more relaxed, although she did keep scanning the boxes. Lee's contacts at the War Office and his own inquiries had brought him no new leads, so there was no other choice but to put his womenfolk at risk, much as it galled him. In truth, he couldn't have stopped them.

At least the opera was good, the tenors in voice, the soprano dying gracefully to thunderous applause.

Private Waters, who'd seen the performance from the pit, sniveled, "Now, that is art," when he joined them at the carriage.

"I don't care how great the art," sneered Sir Parcival into Senta's ear. "You can't dance to it."

* * *

Lord Maitland called a council of war. They were getting nowhere. His house was overrun with carpenters and upholsterers and painters, and his wife had him escorting her and Mona to some social function or other almost daily, but they were no closer to finding the blackmailer or the murderer.

The War Office list of wounded officers sent home at the right time was shrinking considerably as Maitland's paid investigators tracked them down. Most were crossed off as having returned to England via troop ship or, if by private means, in the company of brother officers. Some had long since returned to the Peninsula; a few had died of their injuries. Either way, they were not available to be interviewed.

Lee read aloud the few names that remained under consideration. When he got to one Theodore Sayre, Private Waters spoke up: "That'd be Lieutenant Sayre. They called him Steady Teddy on account of he was so cool under fire. Never left his post, he didn't, that last time, even with a bullet in the ribs. The general had to order him to surgery afore he'd leave his men. He couldn't be no traitor, I'd swear on it."

"He was Miguel's *amigo*," Mona added. "We shared our food and our fires. He would not have betrayed Miguel."

"Still," the viscount said, "I'd like to see your Teddy Sayre."

Sir Parcival stopped humming to Vida to listen. He shrugged and went back to his nonsense rhymes.

Lord Maitland ordered another log on the fire and went on: "The lieutenant may be a pattern card of an officer and a gentleman, but his brother is something of a dirty dish. Sir Randolph Sayre associates with a rackety crowd, gamblers and wastrels mostly. Unfortunately, the lieutenant, by all reports, is still in Bath recovering from his wounds. Sir Randolph could be anywhere. We don't move in the same circles."

Senta was all for throwing a grand party as soon as

the ton started returning to Town and her house was in order. "If it's big enough, we can invite everyone on your list, even Sir Randolph, without being obvious. Mona can sit on the sidelines and watch."

"It's too chancy. And I don't want every loose screw in London in my home." Especially if one was the basket-scrambler Senta might have married. "No, we'll wait. Now that we are so visibly on the town, I think the blackmailer will make his move."

Lord Maitland was right, for a few days later another extortion note was received. This one wanted twice the amount as the previous, and no tricks, or else Lord Maitland's pretty young bride would be reading a nasty tale in the newspapers.

With his pretty young bride not knowing a thing about it, this time Lee was going to make sure the blackguard didn't get away. The last time, the dastard managed to outfox all of the viscount's spies and informants at the inn. A false cry of fire out near the stables had everyone running. The packet was missing when they got back.

Maitland would take the money himself tomorrow to the address on Olney Street, just over London Bridge. It was a commercial district, sure to be crowded at three o'clock, the designated hour. The blackmailer could be hiding anywhere, but so could the viscount, after he made the delivery. And Waters would keep watch.

"You, old man? You can't even run after your hat, much less an escaping criminal."

"Aye, but I can fit in with the ragtag street beggars. Or was you planning on stationing a squad of your footmen, in livery and wigs, at the street corners? Asides, Sheba can track what I can't catch. And I reckon I'm a better shot than any of your staff. Mona's a dab hand with a pistol, too. Had to be, at the front."

"No! I am not putting a woman in danger. Why, that neighborhood wouldn't be safe for her at the best of times. Furthermore, she'd tell Senta, and I'd have another argument on my hands."

So it was decided, without Mona or Senta's knowledge. Sir Parcival would have told her, but he was busy learning the words to "Greensleeves" from an upstairs maid making the beds.

Before the viscount left, he gave orders to both Wheatley and his secretary, Calley, that if Lady Maitland was permitted out of the house, they'd both be dismissed. Or boiled in oil.

At the appointed time, Lord Maitland, in his caped greatcoat, dismissed the hackney at the foot of Olney Street and walked up the block, which was little more than a crowded alley. He tossed a coin to a bald, one-legged beggar and his mongrel, and kept going.

The others, footmen and grooms in disguise who had been stationed in the vicinity beforehand, were waiting nearer the bridge for Waters's call to give chase.

The call never came.

The blackmailer wasn't taking chances this time. He was waiting in a recessed doorway when the viscount went past, seeking the right number. He struck Lee on the back of the head with a lead weight, then dragged him inside before anyone could see what happened, not that anyone much cared, in this neighborhood. He searched the unconscious viscount's pockets for his payment. Making sure the envelope held real money this time, he then emptied the viscount's wallet, to make up for the previous fakery. After dragging his bleeding victim outside again, behind some barrels, the villain re-entered that back door on Olney Street and went through the run-down building to its front entry, on another street altogether, where he mingled with the clerks and costermongers.

Waters waited. And waited some more. Then he began to get a real bad feeling, like he was in battle and the enemy was behind him, not in his sights. He and Sheba moved into the alley.

Urchins playing in the dirt. Passed-out drunks. Mounds of trash. No viscount. Waters cocked his pistol. The ragamuffins disappeared. Sheba started nosing at some garbage, but the trooper called her back.

"No time for scraps, girl. We got to find his nibs."

They found him, by Sheba's nose and the viscount's groans. He was only half-conscious, with a huge gaping wound in his head that bled through the soldier's handkerchief in seconds.

Lord Maitland did manage to open his eyes a fraction and recognize the old soldier. He feebly grabbed for Waters's hand. "Got to . . . get home, old man. Got to . . . return to Senta."

Chapter Nine

*W*aters shouted for help. "Maitland's down! To me, men!" No one came. He fired his pistol. No one came. There was so much traffic over the bridge and under the bridge, no one was going to hear him over the din. He couldn't leave the viscount to go for aid; those young alley rats would have his lordship stripped and bare, if not sold to anatomy class, before Waters could say jackrabbit. In fact, he made sure to reload his gun before unwinding the viscount's neckcloth to use as another bandage.

Waters couldn't drag the much heavier man as far as the main road, even if moving him wasn't likely to finish the nobleman off. Besides, looking at the viscount's absolute stillness and pallor, Waters misdoubted as there was time. He did the only thing possible: he sent Sheba home. "Go on, girl, go home. Get Mona. Her ladyship. Wheatley. Get Cook who's been feeding you. Go on, Sheba. Home, girl."

Senta thought she heard a dog barking. "Could that be Sheba?"

She was seated at the pianoforte, playing for Sir Parcival. He was positive that familiar music would jar his memory better than anything they'd tried so far. He liked the hymns well enough, but kept urging Senta to play them faster, despite the lowering temperature that stiffened her fingers. The Irish ballads were his favorites. He could hear Senta play them through once, then be able to join her in the vocal parts. But none of them struck a chord, so to speak. Neither did the dog's frantic yipping.

"Nah, that ain't nothing but a hound d— Well, maybe it is old Sheba."

It was, and a shaken Wheatley soon came to find Lady Maitland. "I'm afraid this means Private Waters is in difficulty, along with the viscount. I have sent for the carriage, a surgeon, blankets, hot bricks."

Senta was already reaching for her ermine-lined cape. "Those gudgeons tried to find the blackmailer by themselves, didn't they?" She didn't wait for an answer, just headed for the door. "Do you know where they were?"

"Yes, they were meeting the blackmailer on a side street, just over the bridge."

Sir Parcival got into the carriage with Senta. He was shaking his head. "Waters in trouble over the bridge? Troubled Waters over the bridge?"

"Oh, shut up, do," Senta demanded, which had Mr. Calley, who was ducking his head to enter the coach, decide to ride up with the driver.

After a harrowing ride, with the heavy coach careening around turns and barreling through traffic, they crossed the bridge. The carriage couldn't fit up the narrow side street where a mob had gathered. Waters had promised one of the street urchins a coin if he ran around gathering the viscount's men, so they were all there, trying to decide the quickest and least jarring way to get his lordship out of this filthy alley.

Senta jumped out of the coach before the steps were down and ran toward the knot of men. Sir Parcival was right behind her, but he kept going. "Got to see if there's a hotel down at the end of this Olney Street."

"We don't need a hotel! His head is broken! We need a hospital!" She was at her husband's side, trying not to faint at the sight of all the blood. Mr. Calley was right there, with the extra footmen and enough blankets to make a workable litter. They got Lord Maitland back to the coach, his head cushioned on Senta's lap so she could hold a towel to the wound. "So much blood," she fretted, her tears dribbling on the poor man. She couldn't wipe them away, for she was holding Lee with her other hand, to keep him from falling off the seat on the mad dash back to Portman Square. "How can he lose so much blood?"

Sir Parcival looked over at the unconscious peer. "Stop crying. He ain't going to die."

"Are you sure?" Senta asked eagerly, figuring maybe her haunt had a connection at the Pearly Gates after all.

"Of course I'm sure. I don't do sad endings."

"You don't . . . ? Never mind."

Wheatley and a crew of servants were waiting when they finally reached Maitland House. So was the doctor, who wasn't nearly as optimistic as Sir Parcival. "Such a blow to the head can mean anything, my dear," he told Senta. "We won't know if he's left paralyzed or addled until he wakes up, if he wakes up. Then again, the fever might take him. I cleaned the wound as best I could, but all that filth . . ." He shrugged. "It's in the Lord's hands, my dear."

And Senta's. She wasn't going to let Lord Maitland die on her, she just wasn't. Not when he was beginning to care for her. Not when she couldn't live without him.

She sat there with him through the evening, holding his cold hand, willing him to live, for her. Then, when his hand got warmer late at night, and finally hot toward morning, she bathed his brow and helped his man change the damp nightshirt and linens. Mona came and sat with her, then Private Waters and Calley, and still she sat, pouring out her love for him into ears that couldn't hear.

The doctor came again and shook his head. He put on fresh bandages, left some powders, and patted Senta on the shoulder. "You must be brave, my dear."

She was brave enough to tell the man good riddance. "For it's a wonder any of your patients recover if you have them dead and buried before they've stopped breathing. Get out. And any of the others of you who don't believe he'll recover, get out. The rest of you can at least be praying."

So they left her for the most part, except the servants in to fix the fire, to bring her meals on a tray, to carry fresh bedclothes. Mona and Waters did convince Senta to have a nap in the afternoon, while they kept watch. She woke in a panic, that Lee had died without ever knowing how much she loved him. She rushed through the connecting door to his bedchamber.

"There's no change, my lady," Private Waters told her. "I'm thinking that's a good thing. His brain is resting, like. It's the fever that has me worried. Can't get none of the sawbones's powders down him, more's the pity."

"Here, let me try." The medicine just dripped out of the viscount's mouth.

"Don't want to go and drown him neither."

So Senta dipped her clean handkerchief in the potion and dabbed at his parched lips, his dry mouth. She kept at it, dribbling bit by bit onto his tongue until the viscount finally swallowed. They all cheered.

"That's the ticket, my lady, get as much into him as you can," Private Waters advised, handing over a fresh hanky while Mona mixed up another glassful of the healing drug before leaving to feed her daughter.

Senta went back to work, wetting her cloth and squeezing droplets between his lips. "Swallow, my love."

He did, but he also began moving his arms. "No, darling, lie still. It's just Senta, just a hanky. This will help your burning, love."

Sir Parcival got up from his seat in the corner. "Hanky? Hanky, burning love?"

While Private Waters's back was turned, Senta hissed at Sir Parcival to get out, too, if his only contribution was more of his nonsense. "Can't you do something? He's got the fever!"

"I can see he's got the fever, little sister, but I don't know what you expect me to do about it. All I'm any good at is singing."

"So sing, dash it all."

So he did, all those hymns Senta had played on the pianoforte. Their composers mightn't have recognized the old church music, and the viscount couldn't hear them, but Sir Parcival's strong voice made Senta feel better. She kept dripping the medicine into her wounded husband's mouth and whispering words of love into his ear.

It may have been the prayers, or the powders, or even Senta's impassioned pleas for him to recover. More likely it was the chill draft kicked up by a spirit's singing. Either way, Lord Maitland's fever broke and he fell into a sounder sleep.

He was going to recover, Senta rejoiced, if only he'd wake up!

Toward morning on the longest day of Senta's life, Lord Maitland's eyelids fluttered. "If only half of what you said to me was true," he told his wife, who was lying beside him on the bed, "then I can't die yet. Heaven wouldn't be this sweet."

Senta sat up and felt his hand, his forehead, his cheek. "You're alive! And awake. Do you know me?"

Lee struggled to bring one of his hands to the side of her face. "No, precious Senta, I don't think I ever knew you, but I swear to learn."

Lord Maitland was mending, but slowly. He was weak and dizzy, with frequent headaches, no appetite, and an irascible temper at being kept in his bed. Alone.

Only Senta's presence—reading the newspapers to him, playing chess or backgammon or cards, telling him about her childhood while she did her needlework by the window in his bedroom—made the hours bearable. Lee was coming to know Senta, and to appreciate her all the more. How could he have been such a gudgeon as to suspect her innocence?

Easily, since she was plotting behind his back.

A few days after the episode at the bridge, Senta brought up the topic of the attack on him. She closed the book she was reading aloud at the end of a chapter. "I have been thinking, Lee, about how we are going to find the man who did this to you. I mean, we cannot permit a cold-blooded killer to lurk about London. He wouldn't have cared if you died." She shivered at the very thought. "At the very least, he's prepared to spread scurrilous gossip about your brother."

The viscount patted her knee, where her chair was drawn next to his bed so they could share Sir Walter Scott's latest offering. "Don't worry, love, Calley's brought in Bow Street, and we've offered rewards to all the denizens of that rabbit warren of an alley. Someone must have seen something. For the blunt, they'll sell their own mothers." He didn't remove his hand, but slowly started to stroke her leg along her silken skirts.

"That's all very well and good," Senta stated, trying to keep her mind on the matter at hand, and not on his hand on her thigh. "But it is taking too long, with you in danger the whole time. I decided on another plan while you were unconscious." His hand stopped its delicious course. Senta cleared her throat. "This time we are going to do it the easy way, all together."

His brows raised, his hand back on his own all-too-uninteresting thigh, Lee asked, "Which is?"

"We are going to hold that Valentine's Day ball I spoke about before."

"Valentine's Day is just two weeks off, isn't it? You can't get a ball together in such a short time."

"We'll be a trifle late, but no one will mind."

"No one will come, Senta. It's too early in the Season. The roads might be impassable."

"They'll come to see Maitland House reopened for the first time in decades. And they'll come to see why the great Lord Maitland married his bride in such a hole-in-corner affair. I intend to wear a very revealing gown."

Lee had the grace to blush. "I owe you an apology for that, for the whole thing. We should have had a proper wedding with all the tattlemongers in the front pew so no tongues would wag."

"No, no. I had precisely the wedding I would have wished. But then there is that, ah, interrupted honeymoon. You must be aware of the gossip. The ball should put an end to it once and for all."

He stared up at her, as if trying to read her soul. "You know that it will be nearly impossible to annul the marriage once we put on a show for all the tabbies."

Senta was counting on it. "I know."

There was a wealth of meaning in those words, and a world of promises. Unfortunately, Lee couldn't think about the implications. He still had to talk Senta out of this skimble-skamble ball. "It's too much work. You must be exhausted after staying up nursing me."

"Most of the work is already done. Between Wheatley, Cook, and Mr. Calley, there's hardly anything for me to do."

"It doesn't matter. We're not having a ball. It's too damned dangerous."

"As opposed to walking down a dark alley with a known criminal waiting at the other end?"

"Touché. All right, treat me like the fool I was, but dash it, it's too risky."

Senta stood up and put the book on his nightstand. "That's too bad, for the invitations went out this morning." She very properly ignored the blasphemies coming from her husband at this pronouncement. When he seemed in danger of repeating himself, Senta interrupted: "Besides, the danger is mostly to Mona, that she might be recognized as someone who could identify the miscreants, but she is anxious to do this. Mr. Calley had the list of those officers whose connections might be suspect. We invited them all. I am counting on you and your Bow Street officers to guard Mona ever so carefully."

"Bloody hell." The viscount's fists were clenched at his sides.

Senta decided it was time to make a tactical retreat. "It's time for you to rest now. I have to go see about the decorations."

Luckily she could not hear Lee's comments about the decorations and their ultimate destination, since she was heading out the door. She did, however, hear his plaintive: "But I counted on you to stay and bathe my fevered brow."

Senta rushed back to his huge four-poster bed and put her hand to his forehead, which was cool and dry. Lee took her hand, turned it over, and placed a kiss on the palm. "Please stay, darling."

Senta snatched her burning hand back. "I think it's a different kind of fever you're suffering, my lord."

"Well, how can you blame a fellow?" he asked with a boyish grin. "If there is to be no annulment, when does the marriage start?"

"When you are recovered," Senta answered primly, hoping her cheeks weren't as red as they felt. "The doctor said you were to have no strenuous activity. Besides, you'll need all your strength for the ball. Now, I really must go."

"What, and leave me here all alone, Senta? Don't be cruel!"

Chapter Ten

"*That* was mean, sister, teasing the poor man like that. Why didn't you stay, anyway? I even left you alone so you'd have privacy. Isn't that what you wanted?"

They were in the grand ballroom so Senta could decide about the decorations. How could she concentrate on wall hangings, though, and floral arrangements, when her mind kept having untoward thoughts of her husband upstairs in bed?

"Well, yes, I did—I do—want a real marriage. But he didn't really want me. That is, that's all he wanted. Oh, how can I be talking about this to a . . . to a . . ."

"Friend?" Sir Parcival offered.

"I suppose, in a way." Senta was used to the spirit's odd appearance. Now, for instance, he was dressed in black leather, with fringes. She thought she'd seen something like his outfit at a masquerade, complete with bow and arrow. She was sympathetic of his faulty memory, and had even learned to ignore the awful tic he was afflicted with that made one side of his upper lip twitch. And no one else understood at all.

"He never said he loved me," she confessed now.

"He is lonely and bored, most likely grateful for my nursing. That's all."

Sir Parcival did that thing with his lip again. "He was worried sick about you. He cares about your safety and wants you with him all the time. If that's not loving you, I don't know what is."

"He still needs an heir, and I seem to be the only woman to hand."

"I've seen the way he looks at you. No man looks at a broodmare that way. Well, at least you're not crying all the time anymore."

"No, he . . . he does like me, I think. I'll learn to be content with that. Besides, there's too much to do to fall into the doldrums today. I need to figure how many yards of lace to order, and how much satin ribbon."

"Blue," was all he said.

"No, I told you, I refuse to be blue-deviled today. I have to make this ball perfect so Lord Maitland will see I'm no harum-scarum female. I want his respect, in addition to his . . . his carnal desires."

Senta was afraid her companion would be sneering again at her girlish dreams, but Sir Parcival was smiling, making him look so astonishingly handsome that Senta almost wished she were better with her paints, so she could do his portrait for when he was gone. Perhaps on black velvet, which was all the crack now. She caught herself having nearly carnal thoughts about a man—or wraith—not her husband, and blushed. She quickly amended: "And at the ball we'll catch the scoundrel who's been causing such trouble. I just know it."

"All I meant was you should do the ribbons and fluff up in blue. Looks good. This old barn of a place will look prettier'n that grand old opera place we went."

"I know blue is your favorite color, but this is a Valentine's Day ball! We have to have red hearts and flowers, pink streamers, and, yes, pink candles in all the chandeliers and wall sconces. Cook has already ordered raspberry ices from Gunter's. Why, whoever heard of a blue Valentine's Day?"

"Whoever heard of a blue Chr— Nah, you're right."

A few days after the invitations to the ball went out, Senta had an unexpected visitor. Most of her friends in Town knew she'd be too busy for morning calls, so they just sent notes asking after the viscount's welfare. Many wrote that they were dismayed at the dreadful state of society when a peer of the realm could be cut down in broad daylight for his pocket change. What was the world coming to? As for Society, they all wrote that they were coming to her party, with eager anticipation.

Lieutenant Theodore Sayre sent in his card with the corner folded down to show that he had called in person, and asked for a moment of Lady Maitland's time. Senta dropped her sewing—the thousandth satin heart, it seemed—and hurried to the morning room, where Wheatley had left the young officer.

The lieutenant was a good-looking young man, scarcely older than Senta, with reddish blond hair and military sideburns that earned Sir Parcival's approval. He was quite dashing in his scarlet regimentals, his arm in a sling, but Senta thought he seemed terribly ill at ease. Suspiciously so.

She invited Sayre to be seated and rang for tea. "Or would you prefer something stronger, Lieutenant?" She was hoping to calm his nerves—and loosen his tongue.

He sat, awkwardly, at the edge of his chair. "Tea is fine, ma'am, that is, Lady Maitland. I wouldn't be bothering you, never been introduced and all. Not the thing, with you planning a ball and his lordship knocked cock-a-hoop. That is, everyone's talking about the attack on Lord Maitland. And here I thought the Peninsula was dangerous." He tried to smile at her, but the light never reached his shadowed eyes. "The thing is, I hoped to see Lord Maitland."

Senta busied herself pouring out the tea and fixing a

plate of Cook's delicacies. She placed both on a pie-crust table so the lieutenant wouldn't have to juggle them with his one good arm. Meantime she was wondering if Lee would murder her for sticking her nose into his business. Well, her husband getting his brain split open *was* her business, she reasoned. "I left his lordship asleep, but he should be awake shortly. The doctor says he is recovering nicely, thank you, and I know he will be pleased to see a new face if you could wait a bit. We could become acquainted in the meantime."

Teddy felt the urge to loosen his collar. Instead he took a deep swallow of his tea, which was too hot, and burned his tongue. "Agh, ah, that would be my pleasure, ma'am."

Senta was beginning to suspect that the poor boy's nervousness was due more to shyness than to guilt, especially when he sat mumchance after that. Senta asked if he'd received her invitation.

He patted his pocket and turned nearly as red as his coat. "Meant to thank you right off. Honored to attend, my lady."

Another silence. "Are you well acquainted with my husband?" Senta asked.

"Not as well as with . . . That is, never got a chance to pay my respects to him, about Michael and all, being wounded at the time. Then when I got your invite"—he patted the pocket again—"and saw you were in Town, I came right up from Bath. Need to ask his lordship about . . . about . . ."

"He has a great deal to ask you about, too. You were a good friend of his brother's, then?"

"Best friends, ma'am, and proud of it. Michael saved my life when I took this hit and got thrown. He got down in the middle of a pitched battle, dragged me across his own horse, and led me out. Then he went back and finished off a few more of Boney's men."

"So you don't think he could have sold information to the French?"

Teddy's cup rattled on its saucer. "Michael a traitor? Never. He was as loyal as they come. I'd stake my life on it. Did, in fact."

Senta crumpled a macaroon, thinking how angry her husband was going to be. "The reason I ask is that some nasty rumors are going around that someone did betray Michael's unit to the enemy. Lord Maitland is very upset over these rumors."

"I heard something about that before I came home. Headquarters was pretty sure there was a spy at first, but then they dropped the investigation. It couldn't have been Michael anyway, not in a million years."

"But who else knew about the troop movements? I assume they're always supposed to be secret. There's no sense in telling the enemy where you're going to march. The general trusts his staff implicitly, I'd guess."

"I should say so. If there was a turncoat at headquarters, we'd never push those Frogs back."

"But there were other men who had to know, to lead the troops. Michael knew."

"Of course he did. That doesn't make him a traitor. I knew, for that matter. Michael came to the hospital to tell me before they moved out."

Senta just looked at the lieutenant over her teacup.

Sayre jumped to his feet, spilling tea onto his trousers. "You're not thinking that *I* sold out the men! Dash it, Lady Maitland, that's not the thing to say to a chap." He dabbed at his pants with the napkin she handed him. "It's no wonder your husband got coshed, if you go around accusing honest Englishmen that way. I wouldn't be surprised if he finds himself challenged to duels every afternoon. Illegal and all, but to cast doubt on a fellow's honor . . . Not the thing."

Ignoring his indignation, Senta asked, "Could anyone have overheard your conversation, yours and Michael's?"

"I don't know. I was too delirious at the time." The lieutenant thought a moment while he chewed a biscuit. "But no, Michael would have kept an eye out."

"You were in a fever?" Senta remembered Lee's disordered babbling before his fever broke. Some of his rambling made sense, as when he called her name or Michael's, or shouted for his horse and pistol. "Could you have repeated Michael's orders, in your delirium?"

"I suppose I could have, ma'am, but there are no spies at the field hospital. Wounded French prisoners are kept separate, and the sawbones don't need the additional work they'd get, sending our men into ambushes."

"Of course not." Senta changed the subject. "You didn't have to sail home on the hospital ship, did you? I hear they are appalling."

"No, my brother and his friend came to fetch me in Northcote's yacht." He shook his head. "Oh, no, you don't. My brother's a rattle, always under the hatches. He's a gambler, don't you know, not even a good one. But he wouldn't sell out his country."

"And this Lord Northcote"—whose invitation to the ball was even then being inscribed in Senta's mind— "did he visit you in hospital, perhaps while you were speaking in your sleep?"

"Lud, I suppose so. Randy kept popping in to see when we could leave. He was that anxious to be gone before the sawbones gave my release." Teddy took up a poppy-seed cake. "Never understood what my brother saw in Northcote. He's a gambler, even worse than Randy, older, too. Northcote likes to play with green 'uns, johnny raws who are easier to fleece. His dibs were in tune on the ride home, though. We had the best accommodations, the highest-quality horseflesh at the changes. No breakdowns for Baron Northcote. I appreciated it at the time, ma'am, but I do remember being surprised a cold care-for-naught like Northcote would go to so much trouble. Do you think . . . That is . . .

could I have been the one who gave the information that cost all those lives?" Gone was his soldier's erect bearing. Lieutenant Sayre was slumped into his chair, almost swallowed in its depths.

"Not intentionally, I'm sure, Lieutenant. Never that. You'd better talk to my husband, hear what he has to say. Someone was a traitor, and someone tried to blame Michael for the crime. We think they might have killed him."

The officer whistled. "I never bought that faradiddle about Michael's rifle misfiring."

"What the army believes is that he killed himself over his dishonor. Now someone is trying to get my husband to pay silence money to keep that quiet. That's what the attack on his lordship was about, you see, although we are not revealing the truth to anyone."

"You can trust me, ma'am. I'm not delirious anymore. I wouldn't let Michael down again, I swear."

"And I believe you." How could she not, when he'd already put his life on the line for his country?

"What can I do to help find the dastard who caused all the trouble? I'll see him hanged, even if it's my own brother. Lud, I hope it don't come to that. How could I explain to my mother?"

"We do have a plan, Lieutenant, and it involves the ball. I'm sure Lord Maitland will be happy to assign you a part in the trap we're setting. I'll just go see if he is awake yet."

The young man stood when she did, but stared down at his highly polished Hessians. "Before you go, ma'am, I need to ask a favor."

"Of course, Wheatley will show you where to go."

His face went scarlet again. "Not that. I, ah, did come to pay my respects and all, and I knew it was a bad time with his lordship laid up and a ball to plan, but there's something I just have to know. I'm sorry, but I can't find out anywhere. Michael had a . . . a friend."

"Mona?"

"You know about Mona? Do you know how she is? Where she is? Did she have the baby? I've been worried sick. Couldn't get word of her from anyone, and the mails are so slow. I know it's not at all the thing to ask you, you being a lady and all, but I had to try."

"Yes, Mona said you were friends. I'll put you out of your misery. She is here with her baby, a darling little girl who we all adore. Mona is acting as my companion until we get this matter resolved and make other arrangements. She calls herself Señora Vegas."

Senta found her hand being shaken so vehemently, she was afraid she wouldn't be able to write out those last invitations. "You're a Trojan, Lady Maitland. Not every woman would take in a female like that with a baby and all. My own mother wouldn't. I asked, in case I could find Mona and get her to come to me in England. Not that Mona isn't a lady, 'cause she is and I'll take on anyone who says otherwise. She's good and kind, and properly reared. Michael was all set to marry her as soon as he had time to find a willing priest, the lucky dog. It was the war that got in the way."

And it was Michael who got in Lieutenant Sayre's way, Senta guessed. With the wind in that quarter, she'd have something else to work on after the ball. Lieutenant Sayre could be the answer to another big problem if his intentions were as honorable as Senta thought. "Private Waters looks after her," she told the young officer, so he would know Mona was not to be treated lightly, just in case.

"Waters is here, too? Capital! I should have known he'd see Mona to safe harbor. Do you think I could . . . That is . . ."

"I'll take you up to the nursery as soon as you've spoken to my husband. I'm sure you'll be even more eager to help with our plans for the ball when you hear that Mona stands ready to identify the traitors if they show up there. She overheard two men speaking after

192

the ambush, speaking of a Frenchman and counting French money."

"Mona is involved? Just tell me what to do. I'm ready. Why, I'd walk to the moon and back, for her."

Sir Parcival got off the sofa and winced. "Man, that gives me a headache." He grimaced at Senta's quizzical look. "The wonders of youth."

Chapter Eleven

$\mathcal{A}$ heavy rain was falling the day of the ball. A cold, unlucky rain, Sir Parcival felt.

"Nonsense. Rain is only unlucky for weddings. I'm just happy it's not snowing."

Sir Parcival still had mixed feelings about this evening. "Doesn't sound like my kind of party," was all he could say in explanation. He raised his lip at his own formal attire, black fitted coat and trousers, ruffles at his neck.

Senta thought he looked stunning. With his hair pomaded back, her strange guest could almost pass muster as a member of the ton tonight, unless you looked too closely at the cut of his jacket, the style of his neckcloth. For a moment Senta wished she could introduce him to some of the lady guests. What a stir he'd make with that sultry, brooding look of his, or that slow smile that could light up an entire ballroom, she swore. Then again, he'd most likely forget his dance partners' names and insult any number of influential dowagers or tongue-tied debutantes. Just as well he was invisible. Besides, this ball wasn't being thrown to raise hopes in the hearts of every unmarried female; it was being held to catch a vicious criminal.

194

Their plan had to work. With the blackmailer loose, with the threat of Michael's disgrace hanging over them, and his brother's murderer at large, Lord Maitland was not going to permit himself to be the husband Senta so desperately wanted.

They were waiting—Senta was waiting anxiously; Sir Parcival was just lounging about, as usual—downstairs for the first of her dinner guests to arrive, before the ball itself. Senta straightened a leaning rosebud in the Sèvres vase on the mantel. Some of Sir Parcival's uncertainty had rubbed off on her.

"What if Lieutenant Sayre's brother and his friend don't come?"

"Yeah, they could all get cold feet, with this rain in their shoes."

"No, Wheatley's had the men erect an awning from the carriage drive right to the front portal. And planks were laid, then carpeted. In addition, we've had fires going all day in the ballroom, to take the chill off."

"Well, you said it was the promise of high-stakes gambling that would draw the men you wanted, not a hot meal."

"Yes, and Teddy made sure to tell his brother that there would be a lot of wealthy younger men here, too, some of Michael's friends from the Home Guard."

"They'll come then if they've got the gambling fever. There's none such dumber, none such prone to taking risks."

Senta still needed her husband's reassurance, which he was happy to give after he caught his breath at the first sight of his exquisite bride. Senta was wearing a gown made of layer upon layer of chiffon in shades from the palest pink to the deepest scarlet, falling from a minuscule bodice of rose-blush silk.

"Worried?" Lee answered her query. "Why, no. Tonight I feel like the luckiest man on earth."

Combined with the smile he gave her, Lee's words

would have melted her soul if they'd stood in a blizzard. As it was, Senta felt the heat rising from her midsection. And how could she have thought Sir Parcival handsome, when her husband outshone any man she'd ever seen?

Lee was opening a box he'd taken out of his pocket. "But just to make sure, I've bought you a good-luck charm. Happy Valentine's Day, darling." He took out a magnificent diamond necklace, embellished with an enormous ruby pendant. While Senta dabbed at her eyes, speechless, Lee unfastened her pearls and affixed the diamonds.

"There, now you look perfect," he said, standing back to admire his handiwork. The ruby hung just above the low neckline of Senta's gown, in the cleavage of her breasts. He frowned. "Perhaps too perfect. Don't you have a fichu or something? Maybe a scarf or a shawl or a burlap sack, so no other man can get a look at you."

Senta giggled. "The necklace is absolutely too stunning to hide, Lee. Thank you, but . . . but I don't have anything to give you for Valentine's Day."

"Don't you, Senta? We'll talk about it tonight, after the ball." Lee stared into her eyes, telling her without words that they'd do a lot more than talk.

Senta would have pursued the matter then and there—to perdition with spies and supper guests—but Sir Parcival cleared his throat from the window seat. Wheatley cleared his throat from the doorway. Their guests had arrived.

Dinner was a success, of course. Cook and Wheatley would have permitted no less. The few handpicked guests were excellent company even if they were mostly War Office minions or Bow Street officials and their wives. And Lieutenant Sayre at Mona's right had that young woman laughing and smiling for the first time in Senta's memory. The only fault Lady Maitland found with her first dinner as hostess, in fact, was that her husband was so far away from her down the long stretches of linen-covered table. When he did glance her way, around the floral centerpieces, the serving dishes, and candelabra, his eyes seemed to drift to her necklace.

"My, it's toasty in here," she told her dinner partner, to excuse the warmth rising in her cheeks.

The gentlemen took their port and cigars in a hurry, then they all took their places. Senta and Maitland, of course, stood at the entrance to the ballroom to greet their guests. Some of the men went immediately to the rooms set aside for cards, while others took up positions along the ballroom's fringes. Mona sat on a gilded chair in the space reserved for chaperones, dowagers, and wallflowers, with Teddy Sayre right beside her, his sling giving him excuse enough not to leave her for the dance floor.

"You have some interesting guests," Sally Jersey commented as she passed through the receiving line and noted the preponderance of sober-sided gentlemen.

Senta quickly looked around for Sir Parcival. He was sitting up on the raised platform with the orchestra, behind a screen of potted ferns. "Amen to that," she murmured as she greeted the next guest.

After most of those invited had arrived, Lord and Lady Maitland left their post, signaled to the orchestra, and opened the dance. The ball was on.

The music was lively, the refreshments were lavish, the gentlemen for the most part did their duty by the ladies before disappearing to the cardrooms. The quizzes could find no fault either with Senta's marriage or her ability to manage a grand household. Only one old crow was heard to squawk about how the flighty chit was like to beggar the viscount, with all her redecorating and entertaining. No one even listened; Maitland's pockets were some of the deepest in the land, and he obviously doted on his young bride. No, there was no complaint, no criticism from any of the guests. Senta's party was declared a sad crush, therefore a triumph.

Except for Senta. After that first dance with Lee, she'd been too busy to accept any other partners. There were all those scarlet-coated officers to introduce to the debs in white. The mamas and matrons and beturbanned grande dames had to be settled and served. Until Wheatley could leave the door where he was announcing latecomers, the servants needed direction about refilling platters and glasses. There was Private Waters, for instance, manning the punch bowl ladle in Maitland livery, his bald head covered by a powdered wig and his peg leg hidden by the tablecloth. Senta thought no one would recognize him; she hoped no one noticed him take the occasional sip.

"Just making sure of the quality, my lady," he said with a wink.

And then there was Sir Parcival, humming along with the orchestra so loudly that he was creating a cold draft that had the music sheets fluttering and the musicians' fingers faltering. That, in turn, had the dancers stumbling. Senta jerked her head in his direction to get him to move toward the dowagers' corner, where clacking tongues were raising the temperature by a few degrees.

This wasn't what Senta wanted. She wanted to be dancing with Lee again, to be held in his arms instead of being held in thrall by Lord Conovan's boring narrative. She wanted to be whispering in his ear, instead of shouting into Lady Malverne's ear trumpet.

And the suspects hadn't arrived.

The very worst was that, while Senta was on tenterhooks over the absent evildoers, and on trial as a gracious hostess, her husband was on the dance floor. Lee seemed to be having the time of his life with every winsome widow and wayward wife in the *beau monde*. Now Senta was on her uppers. She made her way toward where Sir Parcival was leaning against a pillar.

"Do something," she whispered at him, meanwhile smiling at Admiral Rathbone and his wife.

"Sister, if I could do something, no one would be sitting still."

"This isn't the time to speak about your problems. It's Lee. He's danced twice with that woman."

Sir Parcival craned his neck to see. He whistled. Mrs. Admiral Rathbone shivered. Senta fumed.

The stunning redheaded widow was draped over the viscount like a fur stole, and he didn't seem to be minding one little bit. In fact, his mind seemed intent on memorizing every inch of the lush female. Since her gown, what there was of it, was nearly transparent, his task was that much easier.

"Her name is Marie de Flandreau," Senta told Sir Parcival when no one was nearby, through lips that were about to crack with the effort of maintaining her smile. "But they call her Marie Flambeau, for obvious reasons. She and Lord Maitland were close not too long ago."

"Marie the Flame? His last year's dame? Nah."

"Yes, and she's good ton, more's the pity. Her husband was a *comte* who managed to send his much younger wife and the family coffers to safety before he lost his life."

"She doesn't look like a grieving widow to me."

Senta tapped her foot. "And he doesn't look like a happily married man to me. You have to do something."

"Me?"

"You said you were here to help. So help."

"Why don't you go on over there? She's a stunner, all right, but he married you."

"What, and act like a jealous wife? Never."

So Sir Parcival looked around until he spotted a woman hovering near Lord Maitland and his former *chérie amour*. A refined but impoverished gentlewoman of a certain age, Miss Evelina Cadwaller was the *comtesse*'s companion, a sop to convention and a romantic to the core of her flat-chested, knock-kneed body. She was also as chaste as a nun, not necessarily out of choice. Miss Cadwaller, of course, could see Sir Parcival. Or she would have, if she hadn't been too vain to wear her spectacles.

"Ma'am," he said, bowing in front of her, seemingly out of nowhere, "I can't help but notice you've got the prettiest green eyes I've ever seen."

Miss Cadwaller squinted in his direction.

"Yes, they remind me of the green grass of home."

"Oh, are you from Sussex, too?"

Now Sir Parcival squinted. "I don't think so."

While Miss Cadwaller was trying to decipher that cryptic remark, Sir Parcival asked her to dance. "I know we haven't been properly introduced, ma'am, but would you do me the honor?"

Well, Miss Cadwaller hadn't been asked to dance in more years than she cared to remember, and here was such an attractive gentleman. With a cautious glance to see that her employer was still occupied with the viscount, she batted her colorless eyelashes and said yes. She placed her gloved hand in his. But his didn't seem to be there. She scrunched up her eyes and tried again. This time her trembling hand went right through his.

Miss Cadwaller did the only thing possible for a spinster lady who'd just been opportuned by a ghost. She fainted into the arms of the nearest gentleman, with a smile on her face.

In the ensuing commotion, Senta was there to direct the footmen to carry Miss Cadwaller to a small side chamber. Madame de Flandreau would naturally wish to go along to see to her ailing companion, wouldn't she?

When hell froze over, but Senta was already leading her husband away, to discuss whether they should have some of the windows opened. Did he not think it was growing a trifle warm in the ballroom if ladies started swooning? Should the footmen stop pouring wine for the royal duke who was becoming castaway? And where the deuce were Sir Randolph Sayre and his friend Baron Northcote?

"Don't fret, darling. It's early yet. Creatures of the night like those two don't crawl out from under their rocks until the night is half gone. Come, we have time for another dance."

"I really shouldn't. Supper is going to be served soon, and I need to be ready to hand out the valentines. And Miss Thurston-Jones has hardly danced all night. Really, you should—"

"Miss Thurston-Jones can find her own partners whose feet she can step on. I'm tired of doing the pretty with all of these boring, bothersome women when all I want to do is dance with my own wife."

"Really, Lee? Marie Flambeau is boring?"

He grinned and swept her into the waltz just beginning. "She's not you."

201

Chapter Twelve

Sir Parcival was wrong, Senta decided. He must be an angel after all, for this surely felt like heaven. She drifted in her husband's arms and didn't even notice when he signaled the orchestra to play the waltz again without intermission. She didn't notice, either, how many high-strung young girls in white gowns were swooning as Sir Parcival moved among the ranks of those debutantes not permitted the waltz. Wheatley did, having left his post by the door to announce supper as soon as his lord and lady ceased acting like mooncalves. He ordered the windows opened onto the balcony. Sir Parcival went to see if the rain had stopped.

When the waltz was over, Lord and Lady Maitland led their company into the supper room, which was, in fact, two parlors thrown open and filled with small tables and huge buffets. Every delicacy imaginable was offered, mounded into heart shapes, colored with cherry or raspberry sauce, decorated with spun-sugar cupids. Numbered lace valentines were handed out to all the young people as they entered, the youths from Lord Maitland's red basket, the girls from Senta's. Matching numbers denoted partners for the dance following supper. By some odd coincidence, the viscount pulled the same number as his wife.

There was teasing and laughter and a few good-natured groans as when Lord Hathaway discovered he'd been partnered to his sister. The chaperones smiled indulgently, pleased with Lady Maitland for guaranteeing at least one dance for the least favored chits. There would be no wallflowers at Senta's ball, she'd vowed.

But she'd saved the best partner for herself.

The dance was the quadrille, whose intricacies required concentration and precision. Senta was tripping along gaily, pleased with how well Lee's steps and hers matched, when he whispered in her ear, "Don't look now, but Teddy's brother and the baron have arrived." She stumbled; he stepped on one of the chiffon panels of her gown; there was a loud tearing noise.

"You did that on purpose," Senta accused, holding her skirts up as he led her off the dance floor. "You didn't want me near those men, so you made sure I'd have to go pin my hem up instead."

Lee just smiled and kissed her hand. As soon as she was out of the ballroom, Senta raced to the ladies' retiring chamber, where her own maid would be waiting to assist any of the guests in need of just such repairs. She didn't notice the inordinate number of young chits having smelling salts waved under their noses, but she did smile when a few of their friends asked why they hadn't been introduced to Lady Maitland's most attractive guest.

"Oh, your mamas would not see the wisdom of it." They would not see Sir Parcival at all. "He's not suitable company for unattached females. Too dangerous by half," she told them, increasing by fourfold their desire to meet the mysterious stranger.

While Senta was having her gown mended, Lord Maitland was playing host.

"Sorry you missed my wife, Sir Randolph, Baron. She's gone upstairs for a moment. I'm sure she'd bid me welcome you to our home and direct you to the dining room. Supper is over, but refreshments are laid out there."

The two men protested that they'd just come from dinner.

"The musician's are in fine form this evening if you care to take the floor. No? Cannot say as I blame you—I usually find it excruciatingly tedious myself—but with the proper partner . . ." He let his words trail off like some besotted newlywed. Let them think he had nothing on his mind but his pretty young bride.

"If I cannot interest you in the food or the dancing, I suppose it's the cardrooms. We have two chambers set up. One's for silver loo and chicken stakes, and the other is for more serious gaming. I hate trying to play my hand when ladies are chatting over their cards, don't you?"

Lee was leading them out of the ballroom as he spoke. Sayre was quick to agree, but Northcote held back. "Odd to find such arrangements at a ball," he noted.

"Yes, but my wife is a remarkably understanding woman. Besides," the viscount added confidentially, "she'd rather see me enjoying myself with the pasteboards than with another female."

They laughed, buying his explanation, so he went on: "Truth to tell, I aim to get there as soon as Lady Maitland returns to oversee things in the ballroom. Be honored if you save me a seat."

The two men nodded, happily calculating how much blunt they could extract from the viscount's deep pockets. With all the extravagance they saw around them, he'd never notice. Lee was just about to steer them into the hall when he stopped abruptly. "Oh, but you'll want to greet your brother first, Sayre. He tells me he's been recuperating in Bath. The waters must have finally done someone good, for he seems right as a trivet to me. Except for the sling, of course. I'm sure you'll be delighted to see how he's come along."

Lord Maitland held Sir Randolph's arm so the baronet couldn't demur as Lee led him back through the ballroom. "I'm sure you'll want to see young Teddy, too, Northcote. He told us what great service you did in seeing him home."

Northcote tried to shrug off the praise, but Lee was having none of it. "I only wish I'd been able to do as much for my young brother." A shadow passed across his face, but then he smiled when they reached the rows of gilded chairs. "Here we are. Doesn't our lieutenant look fit? Oh, and may I make you known to Señora Vegas, my wife's companion?"

The two men made their bows, asked after Teddy's health, and made a beeline for the cardrooms as if the pigeons would all fly away before they could be plucked. Behind their backs, Mona nodded.

A middle-aged dandy who appeared to be half in his cups called out to Sayre to join his table in the more private cardroom. Lord Dunbarton hailed the baron. "I say, Northcote, good timing. We need a fourth over here. Cantwell lost his purse and went back to try his hand with the heiresses."

The two men's eyes locked in silent communication, then they split up and took their seats. There were only four deal tables in the paneled room, and a well-filled sideboard of liquid refreshments presided over by two liveried footmen. Play was quiet and deep. Occasionally a gentleman would throw in his hand and leave in disgust, or check his watch and mutter about returning to the ballroom to escort his wife home. Empty seats were quickly filled, as were empty glasses.

The two men were not to know that Wheatley himself stood at attention outside that room, directing the casual gamblers toward the much larger cardroom. Only a select group of well-informed, well-prepared gentlemen were permitted to enter this particular chamber.

Neither were Sayre and Northcote to know that they

were being allowed to win in order that they might grow overconfident, that they were being deliberately separated, or that Sayre, whose penchant for the bottle matched his pursuit of the baize, was being deliberately plied with spirits. The baronet's eyes took on a feral gleam, from the piles of coins and counters in front of him and from the alcohol inside him. He kept licking his lips, like a snake flicking its forked tongue in and out. He barely acknowledged Viscount Maitland when Lee finally slipped into a seat at the table, and paid no attention to the crowd of spectators who had gathered round to witness the play, or the additional servants carrying trays, fresh decks, and cigars. Sayre certainly never noticed Sir Parcival drift through the room and out to the terrace.

The stakes went higher; likewise the pile of coins and notes and markers in the center of the table. And then the real wagering began.

Lee raised the ante and pushed his bid to the middle. The man to his right, the foppish, inebriated Honorable Mr. Bradford, made a great show of deliberating over his move. Lee took the opportunity to say, "Señora Vegas recalled meeting you in Spain." He spoke softly, so as not to be heard at the other tables. Only three were in play now, Maitland's, Northcote's, and one other, the members of the fourth having abandoned their game to watch this higher-stakes contest.

His eyes shifting from the pot to the cards in his hand, Sayre snickered. "I met a lot of señoras there. And señoritas, too." A few of the men around them chuckled.

Lord Maitland went on: "Mrs. Vegas was a friend of your brother's over there."

"They still are, from the looks of things," Mr. Bradford volunteered, slurring his words. "He hasn't left her side all night."

The baronet was getting impatient. "Your play, Bradford. My brother is old enough to keep his own company."

Bradford made his wager, but Lord Maitland wasn't finished. "Mona was a better friend of my brother's."

"That the way of it, eh?" Sayre managed to get a leer into his tone. "Surprised you let her companion your wife."

"The lady"—Lee emphasized the *lady*—"has been a great help to us in our time of sorrow."

Some of the other gentlemen murmured words of condolence, and the play continued around the table. When it got to Maitland's turn, the viscount spoke again. "You must be proud of your brother, Sayre. Getting decorated on the field, mentioned in the dispatches."

"Yes, yes, he was a bloody hero. Are you going to blather all night or are you going to bet?"

Lee ignored Sayre's vexation. "I was proud of my brother, too."

Mr. Bradford, half falling out of his chair, mumbled, "Thought he shot himself cleaning his gun. Doesn't take a lot of courage, I'd say." He was immediately hushed by Lord Sinclaire in the seat across from him.

"I don't believe that's what happened," Lee said. "Neither does Mona, that is, Señora Vegas. What do you think, Sayre?"

"I hadn't thought about it. Dash it, are you going to play? My cards are growing cold."

Lee just stared down at his own hand. "Oh, but you must have thought about Michael's death. You were with the army at the time. There had to be talk."

Sayre's tongue darted in and out. He finally lifted his eyes from the table to look at Maitland. He obviously didn't like what he saw there, for he was quick to utter: "I didn't listen. Didn't concern me."

"Oh, but I think you did. I think you know a lot more about my brother's murder than anyone."

"Murder?" Sayre's voice rose. "No one said anything about murder."

"Did they mention treason then?"

Sayre looked from side to side. All the men were avoiding his eyes. "I heard something, yes."

"And blackmail. Did you hear about that, too, or was the extortion all your idea?"

The baronet's tongue was doing double time. He looked longingly at the fortune in the middle of the table. "I don't know anything about blackmail."

"A man fitting your description was seen in Olney Street the day I was attacked while attempting to deliver the payoff. Attacked from behind, too."

"That's absurd. No one saw— That is, no one could have seen me, for I wasn't there."

"No, but you were at Mother Nattick's bordello that afternoon, which just happens to have a rear exit on Olney Street."

Sayre tried to laugh. It came out as a croak. "A chap has certain needs. Not all of us are so lucky as to have a pretty young bride." He looked around for understanding. There wasn't a friendly face in the crowd.

Maitland was on his feet. "You will leave my wife out of this, you scum." He nodded to Mr. Bradford, who was no longer slouched in his seat.

The dandy, currently attached to the Lord High Magistrate's office, pulled a legal document out of his pocket. "I hereby arrest you in the name of the Crown for the crimes of extortion, bodily assault, and treason. You are under arrest."

Lord Sinclaire on Sayre's other side made to grab his arm, but the baronet pulled away, still eyeing the booty on the table. "What, go from a jackpot to a king's warrant? I'm hurt," he claimed, one last bluff. "Yes, that's it. I'm hurt that . . . that suspicious minds could accuse me of such heinous acts on the flimsiest of circumstantial evidence from an abbess and a Spanish whore."

Major Lord Sinclaire, currently out of uniform, threatened, "Just give the Home Guards one night with you and you'll be singing a different tune."

"And the last refrain from my fists," claimed Maitland, pushing the others aside to land Sayre a facer, then another. "That's one for the money, and two for the blow to my head." He was about to start enumerating the other crimes on Sayre's hapless body, with none of the others the least bit interested in interfering.

Sayre held his hand up. "You're right, but I'm not going to be left holding the bag. Northcote was the traitor. He killed your brother."

"And he's gone!" one of the men at the other table yelled, shoving his chair aside.

From the circle around Maitland and Sayre, Mr. Calley shouted. Taller than the rest, he looked over their heads. "He's headed for the door!"

Where Wheatley was positioned with Teddy and three other young officers from his and Michael's unit. Senta was hovering nervously nearby, awaiting the outcome of their machinations.

Northcote saw the soldiers ready to pounce on him or give chase. They had dress swords and pistols, and twenty years less of dissolute living. No escape there. So he pulled a pistol out of his pocket, snatched Lady Maitland against his chest, and dragged her back with him to the cardroom, warning her that he'd bash her over the head if she made so much as a peep.

"I'm going out the back door," he declared. "And no one is going to try to stop me. One move from any of you and I'll shoot the wench."

"Take me with you," Sir Randolph begged, but his erstwhile companion merely sneered.

"If you hadn't gone greedy and tried to bleed Maitland, you'd never have been a suspect, you fool." He sidled toward the rear of the room.

"Surrender!" shouted Dunbarton, the king's man.

"It's now or never," yelled Major Sinclaire, training his own pistol on the baron, along with at least ten others in the room. "Make your move."

"We're playing for keeps, Northcote," warned Bow Street's assistant director.

"But I've got a woman," snarled the baron.

"Hiding behind a woman's skirts." Private Waters, still in his footman's garb, lowered his weapon and spit. "And they said you was high class."

But it was Lord Maitland who gave the order. "Let him go, men. He's finished here anyway."

The baron inched his way across the room, trying to watch his back and keep Senta between him and any of the fools with hair-trigger pistols in their hands.

The viscount watched, venom in his stare. "Know this, Northcote," he said. "If you harm my wife in any way, the merest scratch, I'll track you down to the ends of the earth. Men, money, whatever it takes, I'll see you hanged for this."

Northcote kept going. There was no noise in the room but Sayre's occasional whimper. At last Northcote reached the glass doors to the patio. If he could make it out there, he could drop the female, jump the garden fence, and be gone before a shot was fired.

"Unlatch the door," he ordered Senta. She looked at her husband in despair.

"Do it, darling. There's no choice."

So she did, and Northcote dragged her out the doors onto the stone terrace, where Sir Parcival had been practicing all the new songs he'd heard that night. As usual, his spectral voice had created quite a draft. As it mingled with the cold rain, a sheet of ice had formed. Lord Northcote took two hurried steps and skidded. The gun went flying and Senta rolled behind a concrete bench. Five soldiers sprang up from behind the potted yew trees and tackled the baron where he lay sprawled on the ice.

Sir Parcival looked under the bench at Senta and shrugged. "Well, I did it my way."

Chapter Thirteen

Lord Northcote was going to be tried, and most likely hanged. Randolph Sayre was being permitted to leave the country, with stipulations, after testifying against Northcote, the actual traitor and murderer. The conditions were that he never return, and that he relinquish his title and holdings in favor of Teddy.

The new Sir Theodore Sayre, bart., lost no time in calling at Maitland House to ask the viscount's permission to pay his addresses to Mona. "I'm not sure if she considers you her guardian, but she is living in your house, so I thought I should approach you to make my offer in form."

Lee wasn't sure of the protocol involved either, and he was positive that Mona and Teddy, Sir Theodore, had already come to terms, but he nodded. Senta, who refused to leave the library during such an interesting discussion, said she thought Teddy was behaving just as he ought, which had that young man blushing.

"I mean to resign my army commission," he told them, "and take up the reins of the family property in Durham. I aim to make the estate succeed for once, rather than bleeding it dry. I know you would do something for Mona, find her a cottage somewhere at one of your estates, my lord, but I can offer her a real home and a life of her own. I can give her my name, which you never can."

"But you told me your mother wouldn't have taken her in," Senta reminded him. "Mona doesn't deserve to be treated like a, um . . ."

"Soiled dove?" her husband suggested, and she agreed.

Teddy nodded. "But now the manor house is mine. If Mama cannot accept my wife, she does not have to make her home with us. It's that simple. My mother is happier in Bath anyway."

"And will Mona be happy?" Lee asked. Senta thought she already knew the answer.

"I will spend my life trying to see that she is, my lord," Teddy assured the viscount in great earnestness. "I believe that she'll accept my offer because it's the right thing to do for her and the baby. Having lived through the hell she has, she's too practical for anything else. But I like to think she would marry me anyway." Senta smiled her agreement.

"And you're not afraid she'll still be mourning Michael?" Lee wanted to know.

"I don't expect her to forget him, if that's what you mean. But I hope in time she'll grow to love me, too, maybe in a different way. I know she likes me, and if that's all I ever have, it will be enough." He reached inside his coat pocket and extracted a signet ring, Michael's ring that Mona had worn on a chain around her neck. "She asked me to give this back to you. That's a good sign, isn't it?"

"Are you sure she wants to part with it?"

"I think perhaps she wants to start with unchained memories, too. Besides, you'll be needing it for your firstborn son."

Now it was Senta's turn to blush. Lee put his hand over hers where it rested on the sofa.

"And what about Mona's baby?"

"I would be proud to raise Michael's daughter as my own. We could claim a secret marriage in Spain or a premature birth, anything so that Vida never has to be stigmatized as a bastard. We'll be living quietly in the country, far from the London gossip mills. No one ever needs to know."

The viscount pretended to think a moment while Teddy wiped beads of perspiration from his forehead. Senta squeezed her husband's hand. "Well, yes, that sounds like the perfect arrangement, except . . ."

"Yes?" Teddy asked.

"Except I shall have to insist on being Vida's godfather, and frequent visits, and that you take Private Waters and his dog with you, too."

After Teddy left to find Mona, Lee and Senta stayed on in the library, her head resting on his shoulder.

"Teddy is a brave man," Senta said.

"Of course he is. Did you see all his medals?"

"No, I meant about Mona. I thought I could be content with your liking me, when I thought you just married me to get an heir. But I couldn't. That wouldn't have been enough for me."

"And I tore myself apart when I feared I was second in your heart, second in your dreams, always worrying that you preferred another."

"But now you know there never has been another, never could be another." Senta cuddled a little closer. "And I think that I could not be like Mona, loving again, for I have only one heart to give."

"When I saw you in that villain's arms, and thought I might lose you after all, I knew my life wouldn't be worth living without you."

So Lord and Lady Maitland had their wedding night after all. It was a bit late in the marriage, and a bit tardy even for Valentine's Day, but no less wondrous or romantic for all that.

213

Senta was in her husband's arms, in his bed, as close as two lovers could be, when she felt a cool draft on her bare skin. Sir Parcival was standing at the foot of the bed. "I think I'm getting my memory back!" he mouthed.

"Good, now go!" She made shooing motions with her hand.

"What's that, dear heart?" Lee asked.

"Nothing, my love, I just thought I heard the dog barking."

Lee went back to what he was doing, which was turning his innocent bride into a remarkably content wife. "Oh, my darling Senta," he whispered, "I love you."

Senta sighed, but Sir Parcival said, "And?"

"And?" Senta turned a perplexed look on the specter.

"And?" asked Lee, even more confused.

Sir Parcival was waving his hands around, twitching his legs, all the while growing dimmer and more transparent to Senta's eyes. "And!" he demanded.

So she shrugged and repeated, " 'Oh, my darling Senta, I love you' and . . . ?"

To his credit, Lee hesitated only an instant. "And I always will."

"Yes!" shouted Sir Parcival, fading completely, leaving only a cool breeze behind.

And "Oh, yes," Senta sighed, before losing herself to her husband's passion.

The last thing she remembered hearing, or maybe she said it, was, "Thank you. Thank you very much."

His wife—how wonderful that sounded—was nearly asleep, arms and legs all tangled with his. When Lee made sure she was covered, Senta gave a sleepy "Hm?"

"Nothing, darling, just that you have made me the happiest man on earth. Now go to sleep; we have a lifetime ahead of us, dear heart."

Someone nearby cleared her throat and said, "Ah, excuse me?"

Lee looked over Senta's tousled curls to see a woman standing at the foot of his bed. She was wearing some kind of leather headcovering, goggles like the ones jockeys wore, and a white silk scarf around her neck. "Excuse me," she repeated. "Did you say dear heart, or Earhart?"

Lee could see the firelight flickering in the grate right through the bizarre figure. Obviously he was seeing things because he was exhausted. "Get lost."

"I think that was the problem in the first place. . . ."